The Other, Darker Ned

That was the nice thing about Ned, Ione had decided. She learned such a lot from him. Usually she didn't even have to ask. She just let drop a doubt or a thought, and he would almost always take it up. She had learned more from Ned than from books or from anyone else. He had come to mean a very great deal to Ione. He, at least, seemed to like and accept her just the way she was.

Also by Anne Fine

The Summer-House Loon
The Granny Project

The Other, Darker Ned

ANNE FINE

Teens · Mandarin

First published in Great Britain 1979
by Methuen Children's Books Ltd
Published 1990 by Teens
an imprint of Mandarin Paperbacks
Michelin House, 81 Fulham Road, London SW3 6RB
Reprinted 1991

Mandarin is an imprint of the Octopus Publishing Group,
a division of Reed International Books Limited

Text copyright © 1979 Anne Fine

A CIP catalogue record for this title
is available from the British Library

ISBN 0 7497 0185 4

Printed in Great Britain
by Cox & Wyman Ltd, Reading

For Ruth M. Marsden

1

Ione Muffet sat, eavesdropping, on the rickety wooden steps that led up from the parched and dusty lawn to her father's study. She had clasped her arms as tightly as she could around her bare legs, curling right over until her cheek rested against her warm, sunburned knees; and her straggling, unbrushed hair, which the long summer's sun had bleached almost to the colourlessness of the dried-out grass below her, fell all around in a tangle, hiding her face entirely, as if she were ashamed of sitting listening there, in the harsh steady afternoon sunlight, unseen and uninvited.

But Ione had no qualms about what she was doing. Indeed, she had shifted herself cautiously and silently sideways along the wide creaking boards, and curled herself up in this way, the better to withdraw from the garden's constant, distracting small noises, and to listen harder to the things that her father, striding forcefully back and forth behind the French windows just above her head, was saying about her.

Ione had thought about eavesdropping a great deal. She was well aware that other people considered it wrong. She herself had frequently been asked not to do it, told not to do it, and punished for doing it. But still she kept on. Eavesdropping came quite naturally to her, especially since her father was blind and she didn't even have to stay out of sight to overhear things, like other people did.

All Ione had to do was keep quiet, and it was hard to feel guilty for just doing that after all. Professor Muffet talked to himself about all sorts of different things. He had done ever since Doris, his wife, had died, and he couldn't talk to her any longer. And he hardly ever realised that Ione was there within hearing, unless Mandy, his plump and ageing guide dog, noticed her wherever she was standing listening, perfectly still and silent, and throwing herself across the room and against Ione's body in a sudden rush of friendliness, unwittingly gave her away.

And for all the entreaties and warnings and scoldings that she had been subjected to on these occasions, Ione could not for the life of her see the harm in listening to other people talk. Sometimes she had learned things that saddened or scared her; but always, thinking it all over again later, alone, when the first shock of knowing had worn off, she thought she would rather have known than not known.

Sometimes she had overheard criticisms of her faults that had hurt her feelings deeply; but more often than not she had already suspected those same faults in herself and worried about them and wondered if they showed. And so it had usually come as an enormous relief to her to find that her father was already aware of them too – that he could talk to himself about them from time to time in sudden flurries of anxiety and exasperation, and then, immediately afterwards, just as if they mattered, but not all that much, bellow cheerfully for his daughter to come and keep him company on his daily walk down to the village.

Sometimes even, her eavesdropping had brought welcome and valuable rewards. Ione recalled with some pride the occasion on which she overheard her father telling his new secretary, Caroline, about the lovely red bicycle he was planning to give Ione for her birthday. She had managed, just in the nick of time, to wriggle out of the agreement she was making with Arthur Heath to exchange her year's savings of five pounds ninety for his battered black two-speed with the rusting crossbar.

Indeed, since Caroline, who was always delighted to drop her work and have a chat about anything, had first come from the Agency to work for her father, Ione had sat many many times just as she was sitting now, under the French windows that Professor Muffet had not even bothered to latch, so certain was he that his daughter had, by now, left the garden. And she had heard much of what she was hearing now many many times before, even if Caroline hadn't. The taut and knotty feeling inside her stomach suddenly loosened, allowing her to breathe freely once again.

It was, she realised with relief, nothing new about herself she was now overhearing – nothing dreadful.

'Mope,' her father was repeating, pacing up and down the threadbare carpet, and making the empty coffee mugs on his green tin bookshelves rattle and jump for fright. 'Mope, mope, *mope*. That's all she ever seems to do nowadays. Every school holiday is turning out the same. She used to run around yelling, and fall out of trees, and get bitten by strange dogs, and clutter up the kitchen table for days on end with enormous jigsaws of the Taj Mahal. Now it's seven whole weeks of moping.' He swivelled around on the turn with an ease born of long practice, and began pacing the other half of the room, ending up dangerously close to the French windows.

For all that she knew he couldn't see her, Ione shrank down further and cradled her knees closer.

'She seems quite happy,' Caroline said soothingly, patting an invisible grip firmly back into her hair, which was piled on top of her head in all manner of gravity-defying loops and whorls. 'She never complains.'

'That's not the *point*,' Professor Muffet raised his voice, enraged. 'Not the point *at all*. It's just not *good* for her. How can it be? It wouldn't be good for *anyone*.' The steady rattling from the mugs on the bookshelves caught his attention at last. On his next pace across, he swept them up and away to the blotter on his desk, where they stood clanking gently against one another instead. 'She never *does* anything. She never *goes* anywhere. And there's hardly another child over six years old around here for her to play with.'

'There's Ned,' said Caroline. She laid her dictation pad down on top of the ginger biscuits and picked a nail file out of the marmalade jar in which she kept all her blunted pencils.

'Ned must be twenty-four if he's a day,' Professor Muffet said, astonished.

'He acts like six,' said Caroline.

Professor Muffet sighed and slowed his pacing down to a gloomy shuffle.

'I only wish Ione would again,' he said.

Outside on the steps, Ione allowed herself a small hidden smile. She could remember quite clearly that he hadn't felt quite that way once. He had fretted about her even then. She had heard him at it. Quite often, in fact, when she used to creep out from under the covers to open her bedroom door, for the comfort of the crack of light. Ione wondered sometimes what it would be next. Would he ever be completely satisfied with her, just the way she was? It hadn't ever happened yet. She didn't know about the very beginnings, when she was still tiny and her mother was still alive; but it certainly hadn't been that way as long as she could remember, and there seemed to be no end in sight to the things he could find in her to fret about. This one about her moping wasn't a new one – he would probably start grumbling about the summer-house next – but it certainly was getting worse.

Above her, Professor Muffet leaned his forehead, for comfort, against the smooth glass panes of the French windows. 'I thought of taking her away with me for a holiday by the sea,' he was saying. 'But we had a holiday last year, and anyway, I'm snowed under with work. We're *months* behind as it is.' Turning, he waved a desperate arm towards the desk which he knew, although he mercifully couldn't see it, was overflowing with essays his students had written that Caroline had not yet read aloud to him; interesting little articles from the history journals that he was still waiting for her to transcribe into braille, so he could read them for himself again later; letters she had not yet even put at the bottom of her huge, Things You Should Reply to At Once pile; and notes she had twice tipped all over the floor and got out of order for the book he had been trying to write for two years. Sometimes Professor Muffet wondered why the Agency had chosen him as Caroline's latest victim. It had been, he thought, a low and petty act on their part. She was the worst secretary he had ever even heard of, let alone employed. Sometimes he even wondered if she had ever heard of braille before he employed her, though the Agency had, of course, sworn she was fully qualified. Maybe she had lied to them, and forged her qualifications, and mugged it all up the weekend before she started with him out of a Teach Yourself Braille book. He knew, because Ned had inadvertently let it out one day, that a lot of her mistakes happened simply because she got distracted by the sight of her own pretty painted fingernails as they passed over the little raised dots. But that couldn't explain *all* her mistakes. Or her forgetfulness, or her untidiness, or her refusal to put more than a 7 pence stamp on anything, even foreign mail. Everything she ever posted for him to anyone had to be brought back to the house time and again by the postman, who had made complaints about her to the County Sorting Officer twice, till all her stingy $3\frac{1}{2}$ pence stamps, stuck on one by one so unwillingly, finally happened to add up to the correct amount for a package to Dar-es-Salaam or a postcard, airmail, to Hyderabad. But she did, he reflected, because he was a fair man, have her skills: and soothing him in his rages was supposed to be one of them. So he raised his head expectantly in her direction.

'She never complains,' Caroline now said again, soothingly. She started filing away calmly at her left thumb nail, which she had just noticed didn't quite match her right. 'If she's happy, what does it matter that she's not doing anything with her time?'

Professor Muffet sat down heavily at his desk, and

cradled his head in his hands. The ends of his prematurely greying hair fell inside one of the coffee mugs on the blotter and picked up some grounds. There was, Caroline noticed, a fresh dust smudge on his forehead that he must have picked up off the window panes. This was not the cleanest house in the village, she reflected, not for the first time. Professor Muffet never saw the grime: Ione never noticed it.

'Caroline,' Professor Muffet said, as patiently as he could over the faint rasping sounds she was making that were setting his teeth on edge so. 'Caroline, think of it this way. I have a daughter – a healthy, intelligent daughter. A daughter who could be spending her time usefully, learning Greek verbs or painting the fence or taking chicken soup to the sick. But what *is* she doing? Nothing. She doesn't seem to read much any more. She hardly ever even speaks. She just sits down at the bottom of the garden inside that silly giant egg cosy of a summer-house of hers, and mopes. Well, there's more to living than just sitting around letting life slide past you, Caroline. Surely even you can see that.'

Caroline stopped filing away and raised her head at that. She would have tossed it if he could have seen her do it, and if all her careful loops and whorls wouldn't have fallen straight down. She hadn't cared for his 'Even you can see that' one bit. She thought she might mention the smudge on his forehead or the grounds in his hair, to pay him back; but she knew they wouldn't bother him. Half the time he didn't even shave, and his ties were just awful to look at, and anyhow he had already risen and started off on his restless pacing again.

'Seven whole weeks. The holidays are exactly seven weeks long.' The boards shuddered violently under Ione's legs, and she winced. 'Five of them have already gone by and what has she done? The sum total of her achievements to date? Two trips to the dentist, and a letter to her Norwegian pen pal. And not much else, as far as I can make out.'

'She did help Ned with his vegetable garden every now and again,' Caroline reminded him. 'Until the reservoir got so low they stopped letting people water their gardens. She planted all the turnips.'

'*Turnips!*' howled Professor Muffet in a tone of absolute despair, throwing his arms out wide, and knocking the plate of ginger biscuits flying towards Mandy, who gazed up at it in awe, as if it were manna descending. '*Turnips! Ned Hump!* Oh, *where* have I gone wrong? *Why* have I failed?'

Ione stifled a giggle and hugged herself. Ned and she exasperated her father in just the same ways, she thought. It was one of the many things, including the habits of eavesdropping and sitting around moping, that they had in common. Indeed, the first time she had ever met Ned Hump, he had been doing both. He had been eavesdropping on her in her own private summer-house – the battered octagonal structure with latticed windows and badly peeling paint, hidden deep within the shrubbery at the tangly end of the garden, which her father always referred to so disparagingly as the silly giant egg cosy. Ione had spent hours and hours of her childhood in this summer-house, quite happy and alone. And one evening last June she had been sitting in there, cross-legged on the flagstones as usual, talking to herself about herself, when Ned, unrepentantly trespassing in search of Caroline, had found her and listened. He had been fair enough to see at once that, in over-hearing what she said, he had taken unfair advantage of her; and partly to even things up between them, for all that they were perfect strangers to one another, and partly because he himself needed someone to talk to so badly, he had shared his own troubles with her, and told her all about his grand passion for her father's secretary, and how every-thing always seemed to go wrong between them. So that although Caroline claimed she loved him pass-ionately back, she could never so much as catch sight of him over a hedge without getting into a terrible temper and ending up shrieking at him.

Ione had listened carefully and tried her best to understand, though it had all sounded extremely odd to her. And this exchange of intimacies had forged a kind of instant bond between them both. Caroline, being irritable by nature, had been a little harder to get to know. But Ione and Ned and Caroline had been the very best of friends for over a year now; and the fact that Ione was so much younger had made surprisingly little difference to anything. It was Ione who had helped Caroline hitch up the zip in her wedding dress when it slid half way down and stuck fast just before the Registrar called them into his office, and Ione who had run out into the street and stolen a begonia from a nearby window box for Ned to wear in his button-hole after Mandy had jumped on his carnation, and chewed it. It was Ione who had helped both of them through the quarrel about whether the wedding cake, which was an ice-cream one since that was the only sort Caroline cared for, should be chocolate or strawberry ripple, and the quarrel about whether the kitten could sleep in the bed, and the quarrel about Ned's having spent half the November rent money on a new gold lamé umbrella for Caroline's birthday.

Ione had given them a double Gardening and Cookery book for Christmas, and helped Ned plant his turnips and Jerusalem artichokes. Caroline had taught her to put up her hair, in case she should ever want to. Ned had told her two mnemonics for the colours of the spectrum, in case she should forget one, and taught her how to whistle. And hundreds of other things.

It had, all in all, been a lovely year. She had never been so happy, as far back as she could remember. Summers before she met Ned had seemed lonely and empty and endless – 'seven whole weeks', as her father would say, of just her father and herself in the large old ramshackle house that he had bought so cheaply when he first married, because the bulge in the front wall that he never saw, and Doris had thought perfect for trailing dogroses over, had looked so menacing to all the other prospective buyers. But now a lot of the days were just like living in a real family. The photo of Ione's mother still sat, as it had as long as Ione could remember, on the piano. But now there was Caroline to push it aside to lay out paper patterns for the costumes for school plays that Ione always needed so much help with; and now there was Ned to knock it over almost every afternoon with his elbow and say, 'Whoops, sorry,' to it when he came in with the large wooden tea tray. Ned and Caroline rented a tiny flat in the vicarage grounds, above the old stables that overlooked the graveyard, and which could be creepy to run home from in the dark. But they only seemed to go there in the evenings. The rest of the time, for one reason or another, they both seemed almost always to be in and out of Professor Muffet's house and garden. Caroline had a better excuse than Ned, since she worked there every week day; but Ned always thought of something. He was always either walking Caroline to work, or picking her up, or borrowing a history book from Professor Muffet, or asking Ione for a pencil sharpener or a can opener or advice on his latest row with Caroline. Professor Muffet never minded – he had been lonely, too, all these years – and Ione loved it.

So Ione sat on in the glaring sunlight that was baking the garden and baking her, and hugged her knees and waited for Caroline to sort things out, as Caroline always did. It always astonished Ione that Caroline could calm and console her father, whereas she could only get Ned into rages. Ione supposed it was something to do with the difference between friendship and love, but whenever she brought up the subject with Ned, he would groan and clutch his belly. Ned hated love. It had, he told Ione, blighted his life, and he was heartily sick of it.

'It doesn't look easy,' Ione would agree, a little dubiously, swinging her legs against the tombstone she sat on, watching Ned chip away hopelessly with a bent trowel at the dried and ailing vegetable garden he had planted there with such high hopes in the damp early spring, out of sight of the vicar, behind the oldest graves which no one ever visited any more.

'*Easy?*' Ned would shout, straightening up to stare at her. '*Easy?* Easy has nothing whatever to do with it!'

That was the nice thing about Ned, Ione had decided. She learned such a lot from him. Usually she didn't even have to ask. She just let drop a doubt or a thought, and he would almost always take it up. She had learned more from Ned than from books or from anyone else. And she had spent a lot of time with him during this long, dry hot summer that had crawled on and on without a single spell of rain. He had come to mean a very great deal to Ione. He, at least, seemed to like and accept her just the way she was. And so, largely because of him, she had enjoyed every single day of these five whole weeks about which her father was now sounding, on her behalf, so very despairing. Ione found it confusing that two people like her father and herself, who were, after all, each other's closest relations, could have such widely differing views of the same thing. For inside the room, Professor Muffet was still muttering, 'Ned Hump – ha! *Turnips!*' to himself over and over above the faint rasp of Caroline's nail file.

But the flurry was clearly over. There was no point in delaying any longer.

Shaking her head, so that her hair fell back and away from her face for the first time since she settled on the steps, Ione Muffet hooked up her sandal straps with one finger, and slipped silently down across the caked and yellowing lawn towards the wicket gate. It was always possible that someone had forgotten an appointment, after all, and that Mr Hooper was now only half an hour behind his schedule.

2

Ione walked through the village by her father's side, still in a daze from the anaesthetic Mr Hooper had given her. She had felt quite ready to set off for home just a few minutes before, when she was sitting resting afterwards, in his hallway. But now they had actually started her knees had begun to shake, and her eyes kept filling with a strange fuzziness and damp. She slipped her hand into Professor Muffet's, and held on to his strong large fingers tightly; but the extraordinary feeling became quite overwhelming, and by the time they reached the short-cut through the graveyard, where Ned and Caroline were standing under a yew, kissing hello long and loudly after a whole day's separation, Ione's legs were trembling so fiercely that her father let Mandy off the leading rein and made his daughter stop for a moment.

'You look *awful*,' Ned said to her, stopping hugging Caroline and pulling all the pins out of her hair. 'Lie down. Have a little rest on this nice, dry, comfy grave. Breathe very deeply.'

Ione lay flat on her back, starfish-fashion, on the tomb he had offered her: that of Martha Cuddlethwaite, born August 5th 1721, died December 17th 1801. She closed her eyelids against the harsh, dancing patterns of sunlight that broke through the leaves just above her, on to her face, making her eyes hurt almost as much as her mouth did. The mushy hole in her gum, where the tooth had been only half an hour before, had begun to throb. The pain was clearly seeping through without much trouble now.

She dabbed at the new, sore gap tentatively with her tongue, which felt huge and clumsy, like a predatory slug creeping around in a vast wet cavern. Her brain teemed with violent, swirling colours. The tombstone chilled her spine through the thin cotton shirt she was wearing; but the rest of her, especially her head, was getting hotter and hotter. She gave the quietest little gasp as her tongue prodded a shade too deeply into her gum, and wondered, for an awful moment, if she were going to disgrace herself and be sick all over the grass.

On the next grave – Thomas Munch, born June 2nd 1790, died September 22nd 1851 – her father lay with his eyes, too, tightly closed. The sunlight didn't bother Professor Muffet at all. But he had heard her tiny noise and screwed his own eyes up more as a grimace of sympathy than for protection. It was the first time he had ever accompanied anyone who was having a tooth out, and he had found the sheer nastiness of the business quite harrowing. Secretly, he had hoped he would miss it. After all, Ione had said her appointment was for three o'clock, and it was not until nearly four that he and Mandy had arrived to walk her home. First, there had been all that clinking and chinking and gathering together of pointed instruments. Then he had caught himself imagining how Ione must be sitting, in that huge monstrous chair, with her head forced back and her mouth forced open, her face distorted and her eyes bulging from fear. He had been relieved when the anaesthetic finally took hold, and she had begun to snore gently.

There were times when Professor Muffet was glad that he had been blind since he was a child, and so missed out on frights. But, more often, he thought that the pictures which swam, uninvited, into his head were probably far, far worse than the real thing. He remembered, shuddering, the soft clunk that the tooth made when Mr Hooper dropped it into a small tin bowl, and he pulled Mandy a little closer against him for comfort.

She dug her chin deeper into his stomach, and began to wheeze.

'You should have that dog seen to,' said Ned. 'She sounds awful. I think she needs oiling.'

He was leaning back against a pillar – In

Remembrance of Captain Flook, 1702–1732 – with his arm around Caroline, who had begun plaiting their hair together, tidily and carefully, two strands of her yellow to one of Ned's dark, because hers was longer. He suspected that she was doing it too tightly, and that she had started way too far up. Last time she had done it, a couple of weeks before, it had taken Ione nearly an hour to unpick them. But today, after her visit to the dentist, Ione didn't look quite up to the job. He supposed he and Caroline would stay plaited together for ever, since his wife was far too vain to have a tuft of her hair cut off later to release him. But it was a hot and breathless day, and he just didn't have the energy to stop her before it was too late, so he just moved his head a little to the right, hoping to loosen himself.

'Keep still,' Caroline told him. 'You're making my head hurt.'

'My tooth hurts more,' complained Ione suddenly, from on top of her tomb.

'Your hole, you mean,' said Ned. 'Your hole hurts. But holes in you are, by definition, not a part of you, and therefore they can't hurt. So you're perfectly all right really.'

While Ione was finding the flaw in this, Caroline asked: 'Why did Mr Hooper take it out, anyway?' Wetting her fingers, she twisted the last inch of Ned's hair into a fine point, and knotted it neatly out of sight with her own two ends. 'There!'

'He said he had to take it out to make room,' said

Ione. 'He said my jaw was too small for all my teeth because I ate nothing but feet.'

'Did he really?' asked Ned, astonished. 'What an extraordinary thing for a reputable dentist to say.'

'He said everyone ate far too many feet nowadays.'

'I don't,' said Ned. 'I don't eat any feet. No one in our family does. Did you eat feet, before we met?' he asked Caroline politely.

'No,' said Caroline thoughtfully. 'I can't say that I did.'

'There you are,' said Ned triumphantly. 'Here, on an on-the-spot poll of two people, you have unanimous agreement that feet are not part of the average household's weekly diet. You are unusual, Ione, in eating feet. Perhaps you are being cheated by your butcher. Perhaps your butcher is a mass murderer, who sends bits of his victims up to your house on the weekly order, banking on the fact that your father won't be able to see these strange cuts of meat for what they are, namely, feet.' He broke off a piece of dried-up grass and began to chew it. 'I'm surprised at *you*, though. A girl of your intelligence should be able to recognise a stewed foot when it's placed before you, however cunningly done over in wine sauce and sprinkled with chopped up chives it may be. I'm disappointed in you.'

'I don't eat feet,' said Ione.

'I beg your pardon. I thought you said you did.'

'I didn't say I did. Mr Hooper said I did.'

'Well, why did Mr Hooper say you did, then?'

'Mr Hooper didn't say she did,' said Professor Muffet, raising himself up on an elbow just long enough to set things straight. 'He didn't say she ate feet at all. He didn't say anybody ate feet. What he said was that all the foods everybody eats nowaways are effete.'

'Oh,' said Ione.

'Ah, yes,' said Ned. 'Well, that's quite different.'

Ione sat up on her tombstone and swung herself around until her legs dangled down over the side. She still felt strange. Colours and patterns still rolled and swirled around inside her head, and she felt light all over, but the pain in her mouth had now settled down to a steady, manageable throb.

She tried to explain.

'He said that if people hadn't stopped gnawing at raw turnips, their jaws wouldn't have become trophies and –'

'Atrophied,' corrected Professor Muffet.

'And got smaller,' continued Ione, ignoring him beautifully. 'And then we could have fitted in all the teeth we grow without their getting all squashed up and crooked. He says the problem is bound to get worse not better unless we all go back to chewing at raw turnips.'

'I thought you were still fast asleep through all that,' said her father, amazed. It never failed to astonish him how much Ione always seemed to over-hear of other people's conversations.

'I think I'd rather have all my teeth pulled out,' said Caroline, and then, when Ned laughed, she shrieked, 'Ouch!'

Ione stared at her.

'Look what you've *done*,' she said to Caroline, in horror. 'You've done it *again*. It's worse than last time. You've done it right the way down from the top. You're completely knotted together.'

'One flesh,' said Ned mildly, smiling.

'Two fools,' rejoined Ione.

'Have they plaited themselves up again?' asked Professor Muffet, surprised. 'I'd have thought they'd have known better after last time.'

'I shan't even *try* not to hurt when I undo you,' said Ione, still cross.

'Don't bother,' advised Ione's father. 'Leave them. Let them stay here. They can crawl together in excruciating pain to Ned's dried up vegetable garden every now and again, and root up a couple of turnips to gnaw at in their death agony.'

'The turnips never came up,' said Ned gloomily.

'Turnips don't,' said Caroline. 'Turnips stay down.'

'Nothing came up,' said Ned. 'It's not surprising. The ground was baked so hard when Ione and I planted the last time that we could hardly get the seeds in.'

'They ruined my knitting needles trying,' put in Caroline. 'All my eights and a couple of long sixes.' She gazed as far round at her husband as she could, and fondly squeezed his fingers.

'It didn't do any good,' said Ned. 'You'd need a jumbo-sized tractor to make a dent in that vegetable garden. The soil is like cement. I kept hoping it would rain.'

'Didn't we all?' said Professor Muffet wistfully, thinking of his ruined lawn.

'They never even *tried* to grow,' said Ned, freshly outraged at the memory. 'They never even tried to *start*, let alone to grow up out of the ground. If there's no water, they just won't *try*.'

Ione looked across the graveyard to the unshaded cleared patch by the wall which they were talking about. It had been so fresh and green and rich and brown, when they had started it. But that hadn't lasted long. And now it was about as unpromising a vegetable garden as you could hope to see. There was nothing there. It was just a strip of yellowing, flat, baked earth. Two deep cracks ran zigzag across the right-hand corner, and a broken trowel leaned against the wall. There were a couple of bent and rusting knitting needles lying about, but nothing alive.

It could be an Indian vegetable garden, she thought. She didn't know exactly what an Indian vegetable garden looked like, but she was sure that, like Ned's, it would look dry as a bone, unshaded and dusty.

She looked over at Ned, leaning cool and idle in the shade of Captain Flook's pillar, with his head on

Caroline's shoulder, stroking her soft, bare arm gently. He wasn't as thin as he was when she first met him, and she supposed, proudly, that since she had given him that Gardening and Cookery book, he had been eating better. He used to wolf down entire packets of chocolate biscuits in one sitting, without even noticing, and still have room for a huge meal, straight after, if anyone should happen to offer him one. They had all been quite amazed at the amounts he could eat.

She wondered what he would have been like if he had grown up in India, instead, depending on a vegetable garden like that one for his meals. He would probably be even thinner, and much darker, and his eyes would almost certainly be brown, not green. He'd look much the same, though. She could picture him easily.

She closed her eyes for a moment. The swirling patterns in her befuddled brain coalesced suddenly, and she could actually see him there, out in the vivid sickening sunlight. He was wearing a stripy, tattered shirt. He often wore stripy tattered shirts anyhow, here in England; but this one, she just somehow knew, was ripped and shredded in a different, a more distressing, way.

He had propped a long heavy hoe over his bony shoulders, and he was standing on the edge of a vast plain that ran away and away and off into a massive overhanging sky that it was hurting his eyes to look at. He wiped his damp forehead with a filthy hand, leaving streaks of greenish caked-dry earth across his anxious face, and then he shaded his eyes and hunched his shoulders the tiniest bit forward. He was peering to try and see clouds in that glaring, glassy sky, Ione realised, and it was very important to him.

Then he turned towards her and looked straight into her eyes without speaking. He looked drained and shaken. Ever so slightly, he shrugged his shoulders.

'What will you *do*, then?' Ione cried out aloud, forgetting in her pain-soaked confusion that the pictures in her head were hers alone, that no one else had seen them.

The real Ned narrowed his eyes at her curiously. She looked quite ashen, he thought.

'What do you *think* we'll do?' he said. 'We can't *starve* to death, can we? We'll catch the bus to Sainsbury's like everyone else, and pay ninety-four pence for someone else's dried-up turnip to gnaw on.'

Ione's eyes widened. She stared at him blankly. Sainsbury's? In *India*? *Surely* not. Surely he *would* just starve.

Tears pricked behind her eyes, and she swallowed hard.

Just then, her head cleared once and for all. She understood exactly what had happened. She had confused, in her strange mood, the two Neds. And the one who had answered her was the real one, cheerful, well-fed and unconcerned. But it was to the other, darker Ned that she had really voiced the question. And she wondered for an awful moment just how *he* would have replied.

'I think,' said Ione, slipping off the high gravestone on to the dried and crackling grasses that scratched at her ankles, 'I think I should like to go home now.'

3

It was several days before Ione saw Ned again. The afternoon in the graveyard had set her thinking, and she had been busy doing something very special of her own. But on Friday morning, hearing his tuneless, lugubrious rendering of *Non Nobis Domine* float in through the lattices, she rose from where she was sitting on the summer-house floor, amid a sea of papers that she had gathered around her, and watched him curiously through the creepers that had become so thin and grey and brittle in the last dry weeks that they no longer hid the summer-house from view.

He strolled through the gate and across the lawn towards the house. With each long lanky stride, he swung a little bright red case up and down. It was the case in which he carried around the examination papers he was supposed to be marking for money, for his summer job; but usually he couldn't even decipher them without somebody else's help. As he neared the study windows, he switched from *Non Nobis Domine* to *Animal Crackers In My Soup*, whistled at top speed and extremely cheerfully. Ione was surprised. She hadn't thought he would be up to whistling yet awhile, unless he and Caroline had somehow ended their furious drawn-out quarrel over the plaited hair. And from what she had overheard Caroline telling her father the day before, during one of their frequent tea-breaks, there seemed very little chance of that.

So Ione supposed that Ned was just putting a brave face on things, acting so cheery and forthright as he passed by the house, just in order to discomfit Caroline, who was probably watching him covertly right this moment over her huge, green, braille typewriter. Ione sighed to herself. Sometimes she wished Ned wouldn't overdo everything quite so badly. She could just tell, from the very way he was swinging the little bright red case, that everything inside it would have broken away from its paperclip mooring by now, and shuffled itself up horribly. Usually Ione was delighted to leave off whatever she was doing, and help Ned sort his papers out again, ink colour by ink colour, handwriting by handwriting, page by unnumbered page; but today she was busy sorting all these papers of her own.

So she stepped back further into the shadows of the summer-house, where the slim, elongated bars of sunlight couldn't catch her and light her and show her to him through the lattices, and she hoped for almost the first time ever that today he would go straight into the house.

Crossing the Muffet's shrivelled lawn, Ned peered curiously through a strange little round cleared patch on one of the dust-filmed panes of the French windows, and saw Caroline sitting as usual curled up comfortably in an armchair, reading aloud, with a half-peeled, but unchewed banana in one hand, and a sheaf of papers in the other. Professor Muffet was lying on his stomach on the rug, scratching Mandy's ears, and listening.

Ned pushed the French windows open, inwards.

'. . . Thereby leading to the more acceptable trade agreements of 1626, 1627 and 1629 between the two sovereignties, marred only by the so-called Carrot War of 1628 . . .' Caroline read on steadily, ignoring her husband's presence, although Ned knew she must have heard the door creak.

Then, changing her mind, she looked up in order to stare right through him as though he wasn't there. 'And the General Vegetable Embargo of 1630,' she added, in a tone of voice so wintry that it sent shivers down Professor Muffet's spine.

Ned sighed. They had been having a very difficult time.

After Ione had left the graveyard so abruptly, leaving them as hopelessly entwined as they later proved to be, there had passed what Ned still

34

thought of as the very worst hour he had ever yet spent in Caroline's company. And given her natural quick temper, which, he sometimes suspected, she made few attempts to curb, this had made it an extremely nasty hour indeed.

First, she had blamed Ned for the fact that they were in the predicament in the first place. He had come to his own defence hotly, pointing out that it was she, not he, who had knotted them together. Indeed, he had had no idea what she was about until it was too late, and she was half-way down to his neck. He had assumed, in his innocence, that she was merely stroking his hair, that these were fond tender caresses that he could feel just above his left ear.

Caroline came back at him with a stunning complaint. If his hair had been longer, she said, she could have tied a neat bow at the end of them that would have been easy to undo, instead of the screwed up little knot she had been reduced to. It was, therefore, unarguably his fault.

At this, Ned had gasped.

Caroline became more and more unreasonable and foul tempered. And as she became angrier, she shook her head more and more fiercely as she spoke, till the discomfort Ned was feeling turned into pain, and his brave winces into bitter howls of protest.

At this point, Caroline ordered Professor Muffet off to Mr Heath's, for olive oil to rub on the plait, insisting that this would make the hair simplicity

itself to unravel. Professor Muffet had come back
with soya bean oil. All the shoppers in Mr Heath's
grocery, backed up by Mr Heath himself, had insisted that, at less than half the price, it was by far the
better buy.

They tried it. Professor Muffet worked it into the
plait, rubbing gently with his fingers. He told Ione
afterwards how remarkable it was that, after the first
couple of 'ouches' from each of them while he got his
bearings, he could tell exactly whose strands of hair
he was handling, merely from the texture. Once the
oil was well worked in, though, it all felt the same,
and rather nasty too.

Caroline spent the next few minutes coming unwillingly to the conclusion that the plan had failed.
She wasted a few more moments berating Professor
Muffet wildly for the fact that her hair now smelled
of soya beans.

Professor Muffet stood by, helpless, holding the
leaking bottle of oil and wondering what to do
next.

In the end, Ned had asserted himself more than
usual. He told Caroline shortly to hand over her
bag. There were bound to be nail scissors, he said, in
the bag of someone who spent so much of her life
caring for her nails.

Caroline refused point blank, kicking the little
green tapestry purse as far out of his reach as she was
able, into the undergrowth around the Merchant-
Truckle's stone angel. Cutting off the end of the plait

would, she insisted furiously, make her all tufty.

Ned braced himself against the excruciating pain that he knew was coming. If he didn't do something, he now realised, they would be plaited together all night. So with immense courage and fortitude he forced his way over to the bag, inch by fighting, screaming inch, dragging his truculent wife along with him.

The pain was almost unbearable. Tears flooded his eyes and he whimpered softly. Professor Muffet, who could not stand to hear these goings-on, at last thought to order Mandy to fetch the bag which he himself could not see. But at the first whimper from Ned, Mandy had slunk off, terrified, and was now hiding behind the vicar's broken lawn mower, pretending not to hear him and refusing to come out.

Ned persisted. Caroline hung back, in spite of the agony, with all her strength.

Ned lost his temper just thinking about how vain she was.

'If you don't give up struggling,' he hissed at her fiercely between his teeth, 'I am going to stab you to death with those nail scissors when I finally get hold of them. Captain Flook's pillar will *drip* with your blood. The Merchant-Truckle's angel will get splattered all over. And my last act of revenge on you will be to cut the hair on your mangled corpse all scraggy before the police come and get me.'

Caroline faltered, then gave in. She burst into noisy tears.

Professor Muffet had done the neatest job he could with the nail scissors, cutting as far down the plait as possible, and unravelling what was left of each of them carefully.

Caroline continued to weep throughout. Ned, freed, stood and shook himself gratefully. He looked down at his wife, crumpled up against Captain Flook's pillar, crying miserably over two or three inches of matted, oily plait.

'You are *obsessed* with your appearance,' he told her sternly. 'It's *disgusting*.'

She stopped crying at that. She started yelling instead.

'*You* were obsessed with my appearance once, too,' she shouted. 'You didn't find yourself so disgusting.'

'Regard for Beauty is a Virtue,' Ned said proudly. 'Whereas Vanity is a Sin.'

Professor Muffet was shocked at Ned's temerity.

Caroline slapped Ned's face.

Neither had spoken to the other since. They had each gone to enormous pains to be spiteful. Ned had taken all the housekeeping money from the cracked china pig on the sideboard, and cooked himself delicious aromatic meals from the cookery book Ione had given them for Christmas. He took great pleasure in eating them, wordlessly, before Caroline each evening, just as she returned tired and hungry from working at the Muffets'.

She, salivating uncontrollably, had subsisted on cheese sandwiches. But she had had her revenge. She had left the fat hairy spider that had stepped in from the drains in search of water sitting in the kitchen sink, untroubled. Ned, who had been mortally afraid of spiders since early childhood, had had to wash all his dishes and saucepans and mixing bowls, dirtied during the creation of his lavish meals, in the bathroom, carrying them back and forth interminably. If he slackened, and left one unwashed on the draining board, Caroline would heave it out of the window on to the cobbles beneath within minutes of being in the flat. By Thursday, Ned was prudently confining himself to rich-odoured casseroles simmered in one pot.

It had been a dismal and discouraging time for both of them. And it was, Ned thought, unfortunate that he now had to start peace negotiations with his wife by asking her a favour.

'I need your help, Caroline,' he now said, tapping at the side of the little red case with his fingers. He heard a sudden suspicious rustling noise inside, and hoped all the examination papers were still sitting neatly in the alphabetical name order in which the Examination Board had thoughtfully arranged them. 'These have to be marked by tomorrow, and I can read hardly any of the writing.' He had been trying all week, he reflected, when he hadn't been cooking.

Caroline raised one eyebrow at him, ever so slightly. Then, with a sudden vicious chomp of her sharp white teeth, she took a very large bite of banana and chewed it, slowly, slowly, till it was all gone.

'Tough,' she told him, sweetly.

Ned shuddered, turned and left.

He'd known she wouldn't respond at once. She had far too much pride for that. So had he. If the Examination Board hadn't been sending him nasty little notes in red printing all week, he would never have come to the Muffets' to ask her help in the first place. And it had been a clever move, making the request in front of her employer. Ned reckoned that had saved him from a goodly spate of wrath on her part.

Ned had been married for over a year now, and he was learning fast. He knew that her refusal to help him out would make her feel mean. If he followed it up by cooking her kippers tonight, she would have to make the next move.

A couple more skirmishes, he thought to himself, a little more happily. Two more days at the very most.

He went off towards the summer-house to find Ione. She could read bad writing too. She had been reading aloud to her father the letters sent to him by learned people, for years.

4

When he pushed open the warped little door and walked in on her, Ione took the pencil from between her teeth and unpuckered her brow to smile up at him. She was, after all, pleased to see him, she realised. She needed his advice.

Ione had been working all the morning, doing a vast number of tedious arithmetical calculations and a lot of hard thinking; but now she had reached an impasse. Banking on all Ned's extra knowledge and experience, she asked him: 'Which would you rather be given, Ned? A pregnant goat or eight hundred and thirty-two chicks.'

'Eight hundred and thirty-two chicks,' said Ned without a moment's hesitation, shifting some of the papers aside with his foot and dropping down beside her on the cool flagstones. 'I would take the chicks. Eight hundred and thirty-two sounds like a fair few to handle; but I already have a goat, even though, as far as I know, she isn't pregnant. Indeed, I made the serious mistake of marrying her.'

Ione giggled.

'Are you two still at it?' she asked. 'Daddy will be pleased. He's hoping to clear his work backlog if you keep it up all through next week.'

'I beg your pardon,' Ned said icily.

Ione, all unheeding, went on to explain.

'Daddy says if it hadn't been for all the rows you two have had since you got married, his desk would probably have collapsed by now. He says your ill-matched temperaments are the saving of his career. He says he feels very sorry for you both, being so miserable and all that whenever it happens, but it's an ill wind that blows nobody any good. He says Caroline becomes a whirlwind of activity whenever you quarrel. He said she cleared an entire month's correspondence off the windowsill in two days when you had that big fight over which of the goldfish to keep. He says he always knows the minute you two have made it up again, because she just goes back to mooning and sitting and painting her toenails all day.'

'Well,' said Ned. 'Well, well, well. He says all that, does he?'

'Yes,' said Ione simply. 'Quite often.'

Ned's curiosity battled with his marital pride for a few moments, and won with ease.

'How does he know she paints her toenails?' he asked, intrigued. 'She doesn't *know* he knows. She thinks she's very clever the way she slips in all that nail varnishing and hair curling and eyebrow shaping in front of his very eyes.'

'He may be blind, but he's not daft,' said Ione. 'And he can smell the varnish. At first, he thought it was pear drops, and asked if he could have one, and was very hurt when she denied having any. But then a few days afterwards he found out, when she kicked Mandy in a frightful rage.'

'She's *always* done that,' said Ned Hump. 'She's notorious at the Agency for being a secret guide dog kicker. Your father is the very first person who hasn't sacked her for it.'

'He thought it was over-enthusiasm for her work,' Ione said. 'She had such good references. He didn't realise everyone was just trying to fob her off on him because he's not choosy. He thought Caroline kept kicking Mandy because she will keep trampling all over the papers and books on the floor. But then he realised that Caroline didn't care at all about that. She tramples all over them too, he says. In shoes. But one day Caroline really gave herself away. She really lost her temper. Usually she just kicks Mandy sneakily under the table. But this time she kicked her half way out of the French windows, shouting, "Smelly rotten dog hairs all over my toenails. Now I shall have to start all over again!" '

A smile of pride and delight crept over Ned Hump's features. But catching Ione's stern, inquisitive look, he banished it at once.

'Your father has exemplary tolerance, allowing my wife to idle her days away in his study, preening herself,' he said. 'When one bears in mind that he even pays her for doing it, his behaviour can be viewed as little short of saintly.'

Relieved, Ione relaxed.

'She really is a goat,' added Ned.

He got to his feet and started prowling around the small confined space like a caged beast, peering through the latticework. All this talk about the person he was quarrelling with was unsettling him. He picked up one of Ione's pencils and began teasing a spider in the web over the door. It was the tiniest spider he had ever seen. He took his revenge on it for the big fat hairy one that was still in his kitchen sink. Pressing the pencil point down just firmly enough on an important web strand to bounce but not break it, he burst out balefully at Ione: 'What a goat she is! I'm surprised you're thinking of getting me another. I'm only allowed to be married to one goat at once.'

'This one isn't for you,' said Ione. 'It's for someone else.'

It was for Ned really, she thought, in a way.

Ione had, in the last few days, taken even herself by surprise. She had decided to do something with the last two weeks left to her of her summer holiday; something to help the other Ned she had seen suddenly that day in the graveyard: the other, darker Ned on whose land the rains would not fall, and

44

whose vegetable garden lay rutted and hard, like bits of broken china. She didn't know quite where the idea of actually helping him had sprung from, and she hadn't wasted much time wondering about that. For once it had come to her that she should, and that seemed so simple and obvious now that she had no doubts at all about it, the main problem had been to work out exactly how. After all, she hadn't much time. Five whole weeks of her holiday had already gone by. There was no time to lose.

So the very next day she had gone into Eveling on the bus by herself, without a word to anyone. She had asked and found the way to the Oxfam shop she had heard all the villagers talk about, across from the fish market, on the Balls Ferry Road. She had spent hours there; and behind all the clutter round the edges – the fancy sequined blouses, and the sturdy winter coats with a lot of wear in them yet, the cardboard cartons brimful of wellington boots in odd sizes, and hardly worn baby bonnets with pink tassels, the trays of kitchen equipment that over-flowed down on to the jewelery shelf, the neatly folded tea towels and doilies and napkins in the faded wooden cradle, the trunk of brightly painted toys, the shelf of slightly battered books and comics, and the sky-blue tricycle in the corner, on which some-one had balanced a huge box of assorted plant seeds – behind all this, Ione had found a rack of free pamphlets, all about countries she had never even heard of and interesting facts she could never have guessed.

There were only forty-four doctors in the whole of Botswana, she read. That astonished her. She thought there must be at least that many in Eveling alone. Almost everyone in her class at school had a different doctor, and Eveling was not even a city. Botswana was a whole country. She wondered if someone had made a mistake in the typing. It seemed a little difficult to believe, only forty-four doctors.

Looking around for someone to ask, she caught sight of a large poster on the wall.

THERE ARE
MORE TRACTORS IN SCOTLAND
THAN IN THE WHOLE OF AFRICA

---

it said, in bright orange letters.

Ione stared at it, appalled. *That* couldn't be a typing mistake. An error in a poster was bound to be noticed. But Scotland was tiny, compared with Africa. Why, Ned and Caroline had driven all around Scotland in one week, on their honeymoon, with no trouble at all, stopping to kiss and pick up pebbles at every beach they saw, and sending off dozens of postcards to all their friends, telling them of the wedding. Whereas Africa was *huge*. *Enormous*. It was hundreds and hundreds of times larger. It was a whole continent, after all. It had at least forty countries in it.

Ione sat down on the edge of a pile of plastic flower-pots and reached for one pamphlet after another. She was still buried deep in them when the lady called over to her that they were closing and she had to leave.

The lady was very helpful. She gave Ione a large used paper bag, that smelled very strongly of chest-rub, to put all the papers and pamphlets in to take home. And during the bus-ride back to the village, Ione drew out her pieces of paper again, one by one, still engrossed.

One, in particular, caught her attention. It had a photograph on the front, a rather blurred photograph, of a fisherman standing delightedly by the side of a rough looking canoe he had obviously just pulled out of a wide and glistening flat lake. He held a large silver-bellied fish up in triumph in one hand, and a very strangely shaped piece of netting in the other. His children were all around him, happily leaping and hopping about, wet and brown and shiny. The slogan underneath the photograph read:

Give a man a fish and you feed him for a day;
Teach a man to fish and you feed him for a lifetime.

Ione found this little photograph comforting. The problems were, she had realised soon after starting on the pamphlets, overwhelming. But looking at the fisherman, she could see it was not hopeless.

Ione pushed the pamphlet back into the brown paper bag and sat without moving for the rest of the journey back to the village. She gazed, unseeing, at the fields and hedges and tractors that flashed by.

She was thinking hard.

These were the papers that were now scattered all around her and Ned. They contained the facts that all her arithmetic of the morning had been about. There were about five hundred people living in the village, she guessed. If each one of them gave her only twenty-five pence, she would have nearly a hundred and thirty pounds. And with that amount, she could buy any one of a number of interesting things that would help someone like the other, darker Ned. She had been finding it really hard to choose, in fact, when Ned Hump walked in on her.

'Suppose we raised one hundred and thirty pounds,' she told him. 'That's seven weighing scales for baby clinics, or a pregnant goat to give milk, or one thousand two hundred and eighty polio vaccinations, or eight hundred and fifty-three baby chicks, or thirteen crop sprayers, or half a candle-making unit, or one sixth of a water tank, or a lot of corrugated iron roofing, or two-and-a-bit-bullocks.'

Ned stared at her, astonished. Her eyes were shining, she was flushed with excitement. She was a changed person, he thought.

'Which bit?' he asked.

Ione threw down her list and jumped to her feet. I'm choosing today,' she told him firmly. I'm not stewing over it all any longer. There's not enough time. So what do you think? What do you choose?'

'I choose bullocks,' said Ned. 'You choose bits.'

Ione smiled happily. 'There,' she said to herself softly. 'That's that.'

Ned took a deep breath. 'In return for all my help so far.' he wheedled, 'and all the help I shall give in the future, spelling jumble sale, and carrying things around that are too heavy for you, will you do me the favour of deciphering all the writing in this suit-case?'

He kicked at it. Again, he heard that suspicious rustling from inside, but again he ignored it.

'I shall leave the suitcase with you, Ione,' he said. 'You have until dawn tomorrow to decode all those essays.'

'Like the Miller's daughter,' said Ione.

'Exactly!' cried Ned. 'Caroline will serve admir-ably as Rumpelstiltzkin, without a trace of acting effort on her part; and I, the king's son, will be back in the morning.' Kneeling, he attacked the catches, and flung open the suitcase. But it was upside down, and his piles of loose papers flew out and up all over, like freed birds. A number of small silver paper clips clattered, unimpeded by the papers they were sup-posed to be holding together, on to the flagstones.

The white sheets of lined paper, scrawled all over with assorted illegible handwritings, sailed around the summer-house, dipping and fluttering, catching the breeze that blew in through the unglassed latticework, weaving and threading. On their leisurely, rustling return to the ground, they mixed themselves up thoroughly with Ione's pamphlets, and dirtied themselves on the floor.

Ned and Ione watched, open-mouthed, in silence. Then Ned groaned.

'Oh, no,' he said, and put his head in his hands. 'Oh no. Oh, no. Oh, no.'

As they knelt, side by side, sorting out the different inks from the different nib-widths, the fat rounded letters from the loopy, pamphlets from examination papers, Ned snatched at a sheet of orange paper from Ione's pile.

'This pamphlet's *scented*,' he told her, astonished. 'Here, smell. It's *Chest-rub*, by Vick.' He sniffed appreciatively. 'I wear it often myself.' Peering at the paper more closely, he asked her: 'What is this, anyway, Ione? "One Hundred and One Ways of Making Money For Oxfam"? How extraordinary. I didn't know there were one hundred and one ways of making money for anything.'

As he read down the list, his face became more and more anxious. 'I hope you're not thinking of trying any of these,' he said sternly, over the list, to Ione.

'I thought one or two of them sounded quite fun,' she answered wistfully.

'No, no, no,' said Ned firmly, tearing the list into tiny shreds before her eyes, just to be sure. 'You stick with a jumble sale. They're safe. Everyone knows what a jumble sale is. If you once start on any of these new-fangled things, like Sponsored Walks and Sponsored Fasts, you'll get in big trouble. One small slip in the planning and you'll have some idiot toddler walking up the fast lane of the by-pass because no one told him to stop, or some old lady fasting herself to death to spite all the neighbours who sponsored her. Oh, no. No, no, no. You be careful. You don't want to end up in Court. You stick with a jumble sale and you'll be perfectly safe.'

Ione gathered up the last of her pamphlets.

'A jumble sale it is, then,' she said.

She knew better than to argue with Ned in this mood.

5

Ione sat back on her heels and admired her handi-
work. Spread over the kitchen floor were eight large
posters, advertising her jumble sale. Each of the posters was different. But all bore, somewhere or other,
this information.

JUMBO-SIZED JUMBLE SALE

Toys, clothes, things, nice food and
helium balloons

Saturday, 4th September

At 2.00 pm promptly,

In the Church Hall.

Every item cheap at double the price.
Very Worthy Cause.

Some were written in big bold letters, others in flowery script. One was all red, another all navy-blue. One had a geometric border of rhomboids and triangles; one had rows of small, bright daisies all along the top and bottom.

It was Ned Hump, in his purely advisory capacity, who had suggested that she put in the helium balloons.

'Helium balloons are an idea of genius,' he told her. 'Every child in the village will be there. I can picture it now.' He sat down on the rather grubby kitchen floor, beside her, and leaned back against the oven door. His face went all dreamy.

'Outside the Church Hall, there'll be a long, winding queue of shrieking, impatient toddlers, and harassed, exhausted mums. The queue will *inch* forward, because each child in turn who gets to the front will take an *age* to make up its mind what colour balloon it wants. Half of them will drop their pennies into the gutter. The pavement will be *a-glitter* with lost pennies. The sky will be *crazy* with accidentally let-go balloons. Children will stand there, tears streaming down their anxious little faces, torn in half in an agony of indecision. Shall I keep on screaming loudly while I watch that beautiful red balloon that I stood in a queue for for twenty minutes, float right up out of my sight; or shall I start whining and pestering my mother right now for the money to buy another?'

He shifted his back slightly against the warm oven

53

door to get more comfortable, while Ione listened, entranced, putting all the tops back on her felt pens.

'And here and there, all afternoon, inside the Church Hall itself, people will scream and start as one balloon after another pops with an enormous *bang*: this one poked by a carelessly wielded umbrella, for it's bound to be pouring with rain outside; that one allowed to rise just a fraction too high, and caught by a sharp splinter in the rafters.' He wriggled in ecstasy. 'Oh, I can see it all now. And by tea-time, all the very little ones, who can't quite talk yet, and couldn't *explain* that the string was tied far too tightly around their little chubby wrists, and *that's* why they were snivelling all the afternoon, will have got gangrene, and have to have their hands cut off. Oh, yes. Helium balloons are an idea of genius.'

Ione smiled at him in rapt admiration.

'You're a monster,' she said, fondly.

She gathered her posters, all of which were now quite dry, into a pile. Ned reached for the one nearest to him, to pass it to her. It caught his eye and he looked at it more closely.

Tucked away in each corner of the poster was a little drawing of a dripping, gummy, recently-extracted tooth. Each of the four teeth was done in blackish pencil, and was nicely shaded, but the blood was done in violent red felt pen.

Ned eyed Ione curiously.

'What nice decorations,' he said to her, casually. 'Beautifully drawn. Eye-catching, even. Quite a talking point, in fact. But why teeth?'

'It's for Mr Hooper to display in his waiting room,' said Ione, proudly. 'It's special. They're all special. They're all made particularly for where they're to be displayed. I've spent a lot of time on them all.'

'Yes,' said Ned, pulling the pile of posters towards him, and leafing through them, one by one. 'Yes, I can see that you have.'

After the dentist's was the one for the bus shelter. This one had a little frieze along the bottom. The right-hand side showed several irate villagers standing tapping their watches, and pointing angrily to the bus timetable pinned up on the bus shelter wall. The left-hand side showed the bus driver and his mate sitting comfortably against the terminus wall, finishing their cigarettes, while the bus sat idly behind them.

The poster Ione had designed for the Muffets' own gate was plainer. It just showed Professor Muffet standing proudly behind a table full of what appeared to be useless, broken junk, selling off his guide dog for a couple of pennies to two small children.

It was a good likeness of her father, Ned thought to himself, and smiled.

The whole of the bottom half of the poster for the primary school was devoted to a picture of the headmistress, Miss Casterpool, being swept up and away from the playground by a huge bunch of helium balloons, while the infants and juniors waved and cheered.

The post office's poster showed a big red pillar box, which had letters overflowing from its fat, wide mouth, and was standing knee-deep in a sea of unfranked letters, packets and parcels. On its square white plate, which gave the daily collection times, Ione had printed in tiny, but quite readable letters: *Collections: 4th December, 4 pm; 27th April, 12 noon.*

'That one's going to go down very well,' observed Ned.

The poster to be displayed on the churchyard gate was printed in spiky gothic lettering. Ione had used only dark cypress green and grey. In the centre, she had drawn the silhouette of a crooked, tumbledown church, and inside this frame she had drawn the vicar, quite easily recognisable from his height and his bad stoop, slinking away from the jumble sale with a pile of toys, clothes, things, and nice food gathered up in his cassock. A helium balloon floated above him, fastened by a short piece of string to one of his fingers.

Ned shook his head in wonder.

The pub's poster showed a crowd of smiling drunkards, all ages and sizes, mostly leaning over the tables, fast asleep. One or two, who were still awake, were brandishing their empty tankards hopefully in the direction of the beer pumps. But behind the bar, the publican stood calmly wiping glasses with a chequered dish-cloth. He was saying, according to the words that floated, in a helium balloon, over his head: *'Now then, men. Pull yourselves together. Time to go to the jumble sale.'*

The last poster showed the grocer, Mr Heath, being held at bay in the street by a giant tarantula that had crept out of a crate of bananas, and now stood in a menacing fashion just in the doorway of his shop. It was a very dark and lively-looking spider. Beneath it, Ione had printed carefully: *You'd be much safer down at our jumble sale.*

Ned handed the last poster back.

'You are a constant source of surprise for me, Ione,' he told her. 'And yet your father seems quite normal. I wonder what your mother was like.'

'Daddy says she was a bit of a sphinx,' said Ione.

Ned grinned.

'There you are, then,' he said.

Ione rolled her eight posters up into a thick roll, snapping on a thick blue elastic band. 'My mother,' she told him proudly, 'could juggle with five balls and ride a unicycle perfectly.'

'I can certainly see why your father took to her,' said Ned Hump.

'The unicycle is still in the toolshed,' said Ione, and leaving the kitchen, she went to find everything she needed to put up her posters.

That evening, Ned and Caroline were disturbed at

an early supper, the first one they had shared since the quarrel, by a furious banging on their door.

Caroline, who had just washed her hair, rose carefully from the table. Her head was swathed, none too securely, in a large, fluffy purple bath towel with yellow ducklings all over it. Ned had cooked them both kippers, and although she knew she looked most odd, she was determined not to let the fishy smells near her hair, in case they became absorbed and she would have to rinse it again. The purple towel with yellow ducklings, for all that it made her look silly, was the only towel they had large enough and thick enough for the job. All their other towels had been stolen by Ned's great aunt from seaside hotels, and were threadbare and half-sized.

The banging on the door got louder and louder.

Caroline jerked the handle and pulled the door open over the bad warp in the floorboards. As she did so, Ione rushed through like a small tornado, knocking over the cat's water dish and completely ignoring Caroline. Caroline flattened herself against the wall, out of harm's way, astonished, her purple turban awry.

'Good gracious,' she said to herself, straightening the towel. 'How *rude*.'

She followed Ione through as far as the doorway, and there she stood, watching in growing consternation, as Ione, who had flung herself on Ned, sobbed and thrashed and howled and wept and broke off from incoherent, furious mutterings to shout out a couple of incomprehensible words, and then fall back once again to mutters and sobs and wails.

And all the time, Ned held her close, and patted her back, and stroked her hair, and brushed the hot tears from her cheeks with his gentle fingers. He murmured, 'There, there,' quietly and firmly over and over again in her ear, looking over her shoulder at Caroline in absolute horror. He had never seen anyone in a state like this before.

It was a long time before she calmed down, and longer still before she could stop crying. Ned pushed her down into one of the deep, worn fireside chairs, and held her hands, when she wasn't busy blowing her nose, and peered into her tear-streaked, anguished white face, and tried to wait till she could tell him of her own accord just what had brought on this tempest of feeling.

But each time Ione dried her eyes, took a deep breath and began to explain, the tears would well up suddenly, unbidden, and she would find herself unable to speak again. Ned, kneeling by her side with his arm around her shoulders, would hold her and squeeze her and calm her down again with pats and murmurs and whispers. And Caroline shrank back further and further against the doorpost, appalled. She couldn't imagine what had happened to upset Ione so.

She didn't want to imagine either. She could hardly bear to watch. Indeed, deep inside, she wished Ione had not come rushing in on them with her grief, or her problem, or whatever it was. Caroline felt so uncomfortable. She wished Ione would go away. Go and find somebody else to cry on. Why hadn't she gone to her father? It was his job to comfort Ione, not theirs. Not hers. Not Ned's. Ione wasn't *their* daughter, after all. She was pretty nearly grown up, in fact.

Caroline thought that it was a bit of a nerve, really, bursting in on them; almost knocking her down as well, and flinging herself on top of Ned like that, for all the world as if she owned him. As if *she* was his wife, not Caroline.

Ione had been getting on her nerves quite a bit these last few days, now she came to think about it. Ned had been spending far too much time with her, fussing around cheerfully with all the plans for this silly jumble sale when he should have been wallowing in unhappiness about their stupid quarrel, just as she had been. The jumble sale was no concern of Ned's. What did Ned care about posters and bullocks and hungry people? India wasn't *their* problem, after all. It was pretty nearly as far away as it could be. All Caroline wanted was for Ned to care only for her; and by the time he'd finished spreading himself out between people who needed bullocks, and people who needed their tears wiping away, there was practically no love left over in him to help end this nasty quarrel that had been dragging on for days.

And Caroline couldn't imagine how Ned could

stand to be so close to such emotion, so close to the bruised and swollen face that Ione was now resting against his shoulder. Ione could have just no idea, Caroline thought, how incredibly *ugly* she looked right now.

Over Ione's bent head, Ned, still quite baffled, tried to catch Caroline's eye. She shrugged her shoulders at him, cold and indifferent. For a moment, an expression of pain showed in Ned's face; and then, just as if he had dismissed it by force, disappeared. He turned Ione's face towards him, twisting her gently by the chin with his fingers, and the look he had on his face as he did so was full of love and concern.

Caroline felt chilled to the bone. She felt as if her world had shifted ever so slightly and left her unprotected. She had been feeling horrid all week: unsure-of-herself horrid, which she wasn't at all used to and which she now saw was the very worst kind. It hadn't all started with the hair-plaiting, either. It had really started hours before that. It had started when Professor Muffet was talking about there being more to living than just sitting around letting life slide past you, and especially when he had added: 'Surely even you can see that.'

That had really upset Caroline. She had thought about it all the morning. She had still been thinking about it while she was plaiting Ned's hair so tightly into her own. And afterwards she hadn't been able to get it out of her mind all through the angry, quarrelling silences, even when she was sitting doing something she usually found soothing, like brushing her long thick hair or buffing her perfect nails. The idea had kept coming back and making her feel more and more uneasy. Suppose Professor Muffet were right?

As she stood back in the doorway watching Ned calm Ione, Caroline tried to face for the very first time, what it was that had been bothering her. And as soon as she tried, it was easy. She knew, suddenly, that there were choices to be made and she had to make them now and the way she chose would alter things for her for ever. Maybe it just wasn't enough for her to care only about herself and her appearance and Ned any longer. Maybe she too should spread herself out a bit. And she could start off right now; after all, here was a perfect opportunity. She could continue to feel jealous of Ned's love and concern for Ione, or she could feel ashamed for her own hard lack of it.

And in a moment the battle within her was over. She felt deeply, deeply ashamed of herself. She hung down her head and burst into noisy violent tears.

'Oh, *Lord*,' Ned groaned. 'Not *another* one.'

He let go of Ione and came over to fetch her. Patting her on the back and nuzzling her just under the ears, he led her over to the fireside and pushed her down in the chair beside Ione's. Then he slipped off to get a bottle of beer from the cache he had noticed earlier at the back of the fridge.

Coming back, he said loudly to both of them: 'That's enough!'

They looked up, startled, just in time to see him flip off the bottle cap and get drenched by burgeoning beer froth.

'I'm so sorry,' said Caroline through her sobs. 'I felt mean about not helping you with all those examination papers. I got you some beer for a treat. But then I walked home very fast to give them to you and they must have got all shaken up. I'm so sorry.'

Ned sat down on the stool, utterly defeated, soaked and glistening. After a moment's thought, Caroline unravelled her turban and passed him the purple towel with the little fat yellow ducklings so that he could wipe his face. Her own hair fell in tangled damp rats' tails around her tear-stained face, and she caught sight of her reflection in the window pane.

She giggled. Ione giggled too. Caroline did look funny, all straggly and bedraggled. She usually appeared so very neat and cared for. And Ned, for all that he had wiped his face with the bath towel, still had froth on the rest of him. Tiny bubbles were popping, one after another, on his ears. Ned was, in fact, quietly fizzing. He sounded rather like a soda bottle that had been left open at a picnic.

Ned heard her giggle, and said sternly, 'Are you going to tell us what all this is about? Or did you just pop in for a bit of a cry and a good laugh?'

Ione blushed.

'It *was* dreadful,' she said. 'Truly it was. But it doesn't seem quite so bad now.'

'Tell all,' said Ned, stretching back on the hearthrug at their feet, and balancing his beer bottle on his stomach. 'Take your time. Feel free to go into details, however insignificant they may appear to you. No rush. My secretary here will take notes.'

Caroline stretched out a foot to kick him, but he saw it coming and caught it. He planted it against his stomach, alongside the swaying bottle of beer, and she took to tickling his ribs quietly and gently with her toes. It was the first time they had touched one another in a week.

Ione told all.

6

As soon as it had stopped raining that lunchtime, Ione had packed up her posters safely in a huge plastic bag. She put two rolls of sticky tape, a pair of rusty scissors, a hammer and a tin of used, mostly bent, tacks in her satchel, and set off to put up the posters she was so proud of.

She was extremely careful. She tacked the one for her own garden fence to the slats on the corner, under the overhanging yew tree – three tacks on each side. She knew that if it ever did rain, the poster would keep dry there, and all the villagers would pass by it on the way to the cottages.

She used sticky tape to fix the next to the pillar box. Even before she had finished, a couple of people hurrying up to catch the post had admired it enormously. The man from the main post office in Eveling who drove up in his van just as she was leaving, eyed it dubiously though.

'Bit cheeky, isn't it?' he asked her, hauling envelopes briskly into his sack, and narrowing his eyes at the little illustration on the poster right in front of his nose. 'This isn't a public billboard you know.'

But when she explained to him exactly what the Very Worthy Cause was, he agreed to turn a blind eye until the fourth. 'No skin off *my* nose,' he told her agreeably, and she agreed that it wasn't.

Mr Hooper had greeted his poster with cries of delight.

'Splendid!' he told her. 'Lovely! You've drawn a perfect lower central incisor. I *love* that dark shading. That's just a typical example of the plaque people will get if they don't brush, brush, *brush*.' He prowled excitedly around his waiting room. 'Where shall I put it?' he said. 'Let me see . . . I know. Up there by the enlargements of dental caries. Everyone stares at that wall longest.'

Ione handed him four of the least bent tacks and the hammer, and he pounded fiercely on the wall, next to the photographs of blackened rotting teeth and above the shelf of *Noddy* books. Little white flakes of plaster floated down from the mouldings in the ceiling overhead and caught in his beard. Ione smiled.

Mr Hooper stepped back and admired her poster once again. 'What a good idea!' he said. 'A jumble sale! We haven't had one since the Brownies went to Florence. I hope my young patients go and spend all their pocket money on second-hand trucks with three wheels and jigsaws with two bits missing. They won't be able to afford Mr Heath's gobstoppers for a week or two. They'll have to steal turnips from Ermyntrude Curmudgeon's allotment, to make up, if they get hungry in between meals. Do their teeth the world of good.'

'You've got a real thing about turnips, haven't you, Mr Hooper?' Ione observed pleasantly.

Mr Hooper thought about it, leaning against one of his rickety waiting-room chairs, hammer in hand.

'I suppose you're right,' he said finally. 'I suppose I have. But I'm not ashamed of it. Most of the people I've admired have had a thing about something. Why, your own mother had a thing about trees.'

'Trees?' Ione widened her eyes at him. She had known about the unicycling and the juggling. But no one had ever mentioned trees.

'Planting them,' Mr Hooper explained. 'Lots of them. All over. She must have planted hundreds of them around here. It seems like every time I ever saw her coming back from a walk with your father, her stockings would be caked with mud and ruined and her hands would be filthy. She was just as bad before she got married. Nurse Hicks swears that on the morning of her wedding she had her little red tin trowel in her handbag and acorn and chestnut seedlings in her pockets. And Mr Heath always tells the story of how he bumped into her the day she got back from the honeymoon and asked how their trip was, and her eyes all lit up and her cheeks flushed over and she said: "Oh, Mr Heath, it was just wonderful. Better than I could ever have *dreamed*. I'm sure I got four sycamores to take!" '

Smiling, he drew Ione over to the window with him, and pointed to the short-cut that ran between Ione's house and the graveyard. 'You see all the young horsechestnuts along that path? Well, your mother planted all those. It was years before she managed to get them all to take, one every five yards. She used to grumble about it constantly whenever she came for a check-up. I could hardly get into her mouth sometimes, for all her going on about it. I suppose she walked down the short cut to get here and it always used to remind her.'

'I didn't know any of that,' said Ione. 'I didn't even know you did my mother's teeth.'

But Mr Hooper wasn't listening. He was still following his former train of thought.

'After your mother died,' he said. 'Your father developed a thing, too. It was about you. Nearly drove us all mad, he did. "Are her eyes straight? Has she got enough hair? Are her feet all right? Does she crawl the way she's supposed to? Shouldn't she be talking by now?" Oh, he was dreadful. He just couldn't be stopped. They sent him home from the pub one Sunday morning, an hour before closing time, he was boring everyone so. They took a vote on it first, I remember. I was the only one who voted for him, and that was only because I was having a hard time building up my practice then, and couldn't afford to offend him.' He widened his eyes and stared into space. Ione realised he was miles away, years away.

'Not that he could see me voting for him anyhow,' Mr Hooper rambled on. 'Being blind. And I might have lost a lot of goodwill among the others.' He looked down at his feet and rubbed the fray of one carpet slipper gently against the other. 'But you were a sweet little baby, even with that nasty rash, so I didn't mind voting for him.'

He looked at Ione, wondering.

'That was all a long time ago,' he said. 'A long, long time ago. You didn't have any teeth then. Now look at you. Having your bicuspids extracted. How time flies.'

'Good-bye, then,' said Ione, on the doorstep.

'Good-bye,' said Mr Hooper.

Ione walked on towards the pub, tacking the poster for the church up on the graveyard gate, and the poster for the bus stop up beside the timetable in the shelter.

At the pub doors she stopped and knocked loudly. After a few moments the publican poked his head out of an upstairs window. 'Go away,' he told her. 'Arsenal's losing badly. Come back later.'

'Can I stick a poster up on your door?' Ione shouted. 'It's for a worthy cause.'

'As long as the worthy cause isn't Temperance!'

the publican shouted back, slamming down the sash-window and so cutting off his bellow of amusement.

Ione unrolled her poster and studied it. She wasn't sure exactly what Temperance was, but she was sure it wasn't bullocks, so she stuck the poster up firmly on the painted wooden doors with sticky tape. Ione switched her satchel to the other shoulder. The hammer was really heavy and she was tired. The afternoon seemed to be going by very fast, and there were still two posters to put up.

She walked across the road to the primary school. She had hoped it would be locked up still, for the holidays, and that she could just put her poster up on the gates without asking Miss Casterpool's permission. Ione had never cared for Miss Casterpool, and Miss Casterpool had never cared for her. But the tell-tale bottle-green mini was parked on the curb just outside, and the narrow side door was open. The summer holidays had clearly ended for the primary children. If Miss Casterpool was back today, they would be back tomorrow, and Ione herself would be next. Sighing, she walked across the tarmac playground and through the side door.

The sick feeling hit her at once, as she had known it would. For every time she returned, for one reason or another, to these corridors and washrooms, classrooms and cloakrooms, she would hear noises and smell smells and see scratches in the woodwork that in all the six years she had spent at the school she had never even noticed, but which now she had left made her gasp with a sudden aching sense of renewed familiarity and of loss.

'It's called Nostalgia,' Ned had whispered to her once. She mentioned the feeling to him half-way through the production of *Dracula* which the Brownies put on six nights in a row to raise funds for their trip to the Dordogne. 'Some people like it. Personally, I rank it only a fraction less nasty than Being In Love. And so I should keep away in future if I were you.' He had peered up through the darkness at the stage. 'Ione,' he had asked in his turn. 'Is that a *real* corpse the Brownies are using?'

Ione had kept away ever since, but now she walked through the corridors, raising herself on her toes to peep through all the small, square glass panes set high in the doors, until she found Miss Casterpool in the infants' classroom, sorting flash cards. Ione remembered flash cards vividly. A rush of revulsion swept her other more delicate feelings away, and she shuddered slightly as she came through the door.

Miss Casterpool did not look up from the flash cards.

'Can I put this poster up on the playground gates?' Ione asked her politely.

'May I,' corrected Miss Casterpool, still not looking up.

Ione sighed. She found May-I grown ups trying. It was, she recalled, one of the reasons she had never cared for Miss Casterpool.

'*May* I, then?' she asked.

'No,' said Miss Casterpool, beginning a new pile for short vowel sounds, 'you may not. The playground gates were not designed for posters.'

'It's a very worthy cause,' said Ione. 'It's for bullocks to pull ploughs to till the soil to plant seeds to grow food for hungry people.'

As she spoke, she had a sudden blinding image of the other, darker Ned. He was sitting on his heels on the edge of his land, head in hands, rocking his body slowly from side to side. A sense of panic gripped Ione. She could see that he was getting desperate.

'A very worthy cause,' she repeated.

'It would set a dangerous precedent,' warned Miss Casterpool, laying all the flash cards with words ending in silent 'e' on one side.

'Dangerous?'

'All manner of people, seeing your poster on the playground gates, might come to me seeking permission to put up their own posters as well.'

'So?' said Ione.

Miss Casterpool looked up from the flash cards for the very first time. She studied Ione's face closely.

'Are you being insolent, Ione?' she asked. Not being sure whether she was or not, was, Miss Casterpool recalled, one of the reasons she had never cared for Ione.

'No, Miss Casterpool,' said Ione, falling back promptly on the dumb, bland tone of voice she knew from experience was the only one Miss Casterpool could take. 'I'm not, really.'

'The gate is not a notice-board,' said Miss Casterpool frostily. 'I consider the subject closed. And, Ione, please carry that other box of flash cards to the office for me on your way out.'

Ione stood perfectly still for a moment. She was willing every single part of her not to feel five years old again, or act that way. And as soon as she was sure she was quite ready, she said calmly:

'No. No, I won't. It might set a dangerous precedent. All manner of people, seeing me carrying your flash card box to the office, might want to carry it too.'

She walked out. With immense self-control she pulled the door to behind her, as quietly as she could. Even if the Brownies put on *Frankenstein*, with real lightning next year, they would never get her inside the primary school again.

She ought to have stopped right then, she knew. She realised she was getting into a state. But the grocer's was on the way home, and this was an important poster. Everybody in the village shopped from Mr Heath.

Ione pushed open the door. Above her head the little brass bell jangled furiously. Mr Heath looked up and smiled at her as she came in. He held his young son Geoffrey, who was grizzling softly, in one crooked arm, and with the other he was tipping gobstoppers from a brown package into an almost empty glass jar. The new gobstoppers, Ione noticed, were neither as large nor as colourful as the ones at the very bottom of the jar he was refilling, but he had not changed the price on the label. She reminded herself not to buy gobstoppers for a while.

'Please will you put this poster up in your window?' she asked him.

'I don't take posters, Ione,' he said. 'They cut out the light.'

'But I made it for you especially,' she told him, slipping her satchel off her shoulder on to the floor and unrolling the poster to show him. 'It's for a worthy cause and it will only have to be up for a week.'

'I don't take posters,' he repeated.

'Please,' she pleaded.

She was beginning to feel queasy, and her voice trembled slightly. 'It's to help hungry people to grow their own food in somewhere like India.'

'Are there any hungry people left in India?' he asked nastily, shifting Geoffrey, who had begun to cry louder, from one arm to the other. 'I thought they were all over here, pinching our jobs.'

'Over half the people in the world don't get enough to eat,' said Ione, close to tears. 'They're not all over here. And if we could only help them to start growing enough of their own food, they wouldn't want to come, would they?'

'They could grow food if they tried,' Mr Heath said. 'They're just too lazy. They just lie about in the sun all day and wait for fools like us to send it. And then they just waste it. I've heard about all that thieving and waste.'

He put his son down on the counter. But Geoffrey immediately began to scream and Mr Heath was forced to pick him up again almost at once.

Ione tried to keep her temper.

'There's bound to be a bit of thieving if they're hungry,' she told him. 'You'd steal if you were starving, wouldn't you? Anybody would. And they don't so much waste things as not know how to make the very best use of them, not having ever seen them before. Nobody would know how to mend a tractor if they'd only ever had a bicycle before. That's why sometimes it's better to give them the things they're used to. Like bullocks. We're going to buy them a bullock with the money from the jumble sale. Bullocks are very sturdy animals. They can pull ploughs and pull water out of wells, and you can breed them to get more. They're better than tractors really for some people.'

Mr Heath screwed the top back on his jar of gobstoppers and shifted Geoffrey back to the other arm. He had had a very bad day. Geoffrey had kept him up all the night before with his crying, and was probably going to do the same tonight. He had mouth ulcers. And Mr Heath had a headache. He didn't quite know why he was picking an argument with Ione. All he really wanted was for her to go away and leave him in peace, taking her poster with her.

'You're silly,' he told her. 'You're crazy. What do you want to bother about all those people for?

They're not your problem. Why don't you act normal? Why don't you run around and enjoy yourself in the last few days of your summer holidays, like a sensible girl? Get a bit of colour into your cheeks. If there's that many of them starving over there, one bullock isn't going to do much good, is it?'

'It would help quite a few people,' Ione argued. 'Several families could share it. They're better at sharing things than some of us are.'

She looked at him, meaningfully, over the counter.

Mr Heath became irritated with Ione. He stepped out from behind the scales and began to steer her, not very gently, towards the door. But Geoffrey began to bellow loudly and Mr Heath lost his temper. Since Geoffrey was too young to yell at, he turned on Ione instead.

'You clear off,' he shouted at her. 'And don't come back with any more posters, either. You're as bad as your mother was, you are, with all your notions. She seemed to think she could turn the whole county back into a forest, and you think you can feed the world. Go on. Off you go. Clear off home.'

Ione shook her shoulders free from his grip. She turned to face him again, her eyes wide with fury. All the blood had left her cheeks. She looked very much older to him suddenly, and very, very white.

'I'm *proud* of my mother,' she said in a voice

so choked with anger that he hardly would have recognised it as hers, 'whatever *you* say about her. And I feel sorry for your Geoffrey. Because if you were *my* father I would find it very difficult to be proud of *you*. And I shall never, never, *ever* shop here again.'

'*Good*,' said Mr Heath, and he slammed the door behind her.

7

She had run home, enraged as never before. She hurtled through the front door and collided with her father, who was hopelessly rooting around on the floor of the hall cupboard on his hands and knees, trying to find a shopping bag. It was time for Mandy's walk and Professor Muffet wanted to pick up a few groceries from Mr Heath on the way back.

'You can't shop there any more,' Ione told him, breathless from her run home.

She told him what had happened.

Ione's father listened to her jumbled account of the afternoon with a serious expression on his face. And as soon as she had finished he began pacing up and down the hall rug, just missing the wide open cupboard door on each turn, looking very unhappy indeed. Ione wondered if he were worrying about where they would buy their groceries in future. Until now she hadn't given that any thought herself. But when he turned to face her, she saw with a sinking feeling that his face was set graver than that – graver than groceries.

He stopped his pacing and stood in front of her.

'You will have to go straight back there and apologise,' he said.

Ione was astonished. Hadn't he been listening to her properly? Hadn't he understood? He should have understood. He knew how important the jumble sale was to her now. She had told him all about the posters and the bullocks and the helium balloons over supper. He had seemed really pleased about it. Delighted, in fact. And now he had turned on her, just like that, without a word of warning. Ione was bitterly hurt, and very, very angry. After all, it was he who had gone on to Caroline so about her not doing things. He hadn't realised that she'd been listening, of course – and this was hardly the time to mention it – but that was surely beside the point. He had let her down. Worse than that, not only had he let her down, but he also expected her to go out again, in the dark, when she was tired out from all her doing things, to apologise for doing them. It was all so unfair.

'You'll have to say you're sorry,' he said again.

Ione sat down hard on the bottom stair and stamped her feet wildly.

'Why *should* I?' she shouted. 'Why *should* I? He's a *pig*. He's thoughtless and selfish and *rude*.

He'd let Ned Hump starve to death right in front of his eyes. He was *hateful*. I *hate* him. I'll *never* go in there again. I'd rather die than apologise to *him*.'

'You *have* to,' Professor Muffet said simply. 'You *have* to.' He sat beside his daughter on the stairs and took her hand in his. It was shaking with anger and felt soft and cold. He squeezed it several times, but Ione was far too upset and shaken to respond.

'Listen,' he said to her when he thought he had allowed her sufficient time to calm down. 'Listen, Ione. You're being unfair to Mr Heath. He wouldn't let Ned starve to death in front of his eyes – or anybody else for that matter – you know he wouldn't.'

'Why won't he help me get my bullock, then?'

'Because he doesn't see the connection between the two too clearly, that's why. He isn't cruel. He just isn't as wrapped up in it all as you are. If everyone had a thing about raising money for the other half of the world, no one would ever sculpt or paint or even learn to ride a unicycle. They'd all be out there planting soya beans and running Oxfam shops.'

'I suppose so,' said Ione, ruefully. 'But I still don't see why I have to say I'm sorry to him. He was far ruder than I was.'

'He may have been ruder to you than you were to him,' said Professor Muffet, 'but you hurt him much, much more. You said that if he was your father, you wouldn't be proud of him. That's an awful thing to say. He must be feeling dreadful now. You could hardly have chosen anything more devastating to say.' He squeezed her hand again. 'So, you see,' he said. 'You have to go back. You have to go and tell him you were wrong.'

'I wasn't wrong,' said Ione. 'If he was my father, I wouldn't be proud of him. And I'm not going.'

Professor Muffet let go of her hand. He stood up. He could see he was getting nowhere with her. She was as stubborn as her mother.

'Ione,' he said. 'I'm giving you till breakfast time tomorrow to think of one nice thing about Mr Heath that a daughter of his could be proud of him for. And I'm giving you till lunchtime tomorrow to say you're sorry to him. And if you can't tell me at lunch tomorrow that you've tried to make your peace with Mr Heath, then you can just cancel your jumble sale. Because if by doing some good for people you don't know, you just hurt and despise the people around you whom you do know, then you'd better not do any good at all. You'd better wait a few years till you're old enough either to do something useful without making enemies, or not to mind seeing the people you antagonise cross the street when they see you coming.'

Ione stared at him. She was so taken aback she couldn't speak. First he wanted her to do things, then he threatened to stop her. Wouldn't she *ever* get things right? She opened her mouth a couple of times to argue, but she couldn't think of anything to say.

Suddenly the whole day flooded in on her: the hours she had spent on the posters; the miles she had walked putting them up; all that talk about her mother; Miss Casterpool's niggliness; her row with Mr Heath; and now her own father was against her, or so it seemed. If this was what came of listening to other people talk about you, then she would have no more of it. She would never eavesdrop again.

'Well?' he asked her sternly. 'Well?'

Tears pricked behind Ione's eyes and she clenched her fists till the knuckles paled. She was ready to fly at him. She wanted to hit him, hard. He wouldn't see it coming and he could never hit her back.

Ione made for the door as fast as she could. She ran off, out across the lawn towards the gate. She left the front door swinging.

Professor Muffet felt the draught but he did not move to close the door. Instead he sat down on the bottom stair again and put his head in his hands.

As soon as she was sure that the shouting was over, Mandy crept out from where she had been hiding, deep in the hall cupboard. She wriggled close and licked Professor Muffet's fingers wetly; but he was feeling far too shaken to respond.

'He's right, you know,' said Ned, lying flat on his back on the hearth-rug with his beer bottle just beside his left ear. 'Maddening as it may be to you, young passionate and idealistic as you are, he's perfectly right.'

He was becoming expansive, Ione noticed. It had taken her some time to tell everything. He was on his third pint.

'If he were to let you get away with it,' Ned went on, 'you'd turn into a nasty prig. It's the major pitfall for people who have worthy causes. An awful lot of them fall into it.'

'You don't fall into a pitfall,' quibbled Caroline. 'A pitfall falls on you.'

Ione smiled. She didn't mind Caroline's niggling. It was a whole lot different from Miss Casterpool's. Ione felt much happier now. She realised that none of it seemed so bad any more. Not everything was as spoiled as she had believed. She could see she had been horrid to poor Mr Heath. She could even imagine making friends with him again, if he would let her.

'Next thing you know,' Ned said, waving his beer bottle around in the air, and spilling it, 'you'll despise all of us. Your father for writing Useless Old History Books About Food Riots that will never feed anyone, me for not being able to read anyone's writing, and Caroline for being totally indifferent to the world's ills just so long as her nails are beautifully polished and her coiffure is perfection.'

Caroline blushed and inspected her nails. They were, indeed, beautifully polished; but she had made a lot of decisions in the last couple of hours. It would have been hard for anyone to listen to Ione's tale without being impressed by her determination. And

Caroline had been very impressed indeed. Ione had never been at all like that before. If someone like Ione could suddenly just show a whole other side of herself that no one had ever suspected was there before, then maybe Caroline could too.

Caroline didn't mind Ned's teasing. She might even slip off and sort her hair out in a while. But she would surprise Ned in the long run. Ned would see.

Ione slid out of the armchair. 'I'd better go home now,' she said. 'And thank you both very much.'

'You're welcome,' said Ned. 'Any time you feel hysterical you're to drop in, isn't she, Caroline?'

Caroline didn't answer. She was absorbed, trying to brush out all the knots that had dried in her long silky hair.

Ione walked slowly home in the gathering dark. There was nobody else about. It must be pretty late, she thought to herself. She was tired out.

She could hear, from further along the village street, a rattling of keys and chains. Just at that moment, a lamp was switched on in one of the cottages, lighting up part of the pavement. She saw Mr Heath there, outside his shop, with a bunch of keys in his hand. And as she drew nearer, under the street lamp, he saw her too.

He started. Then he continued to look in her direction for a moment, but gave no further sign that he had seen her. His face was closed and expressionless in the queer half-lighting.

Casually, he began whistling softly to himself. And although his house, Ione knew, was in the direction she herself was coming from, and he ought really to walk past her, instead he walked hurriedly across the street away from her, and disappeared down an alley that ran between the post office and the cottages.

It was a long time before Ione fell asleep that night. And by the time Mr Heath came to open up his shop at half-past eight the following morning, she had already been waiting for him for twenty minutes.

8

On Thursday night it rained. Ione was woken by
the noise of it, splattering and beating against the
small square panes of glass above her head, sheeting
off the blocked and rusted gutters just outside her
window, like syrup off a giant wooden spoon, and
falling in heavy uneven splashes on to the flooded
paths below. The slim, shiny, rain-soaked branches
of the prunus leaned so far over that they scratched
and tapped against the sodden house walls; and the
ill-fitting lid on the garden water-butt below began
to thud gently and rhythmically as the rising wind
lifted it and then let it fall, over and over again.

Ione lay on her back, with her arms crooked back
underneath her head, staring up at the ceiling
through the darkness. It's been a long time, she told
herself happily. A very long time.

She was filled with an enormous sense of relief.

The long, long summer was over. The sheer wetness of everything outside would drive it away within hours. The ground would soften, the grass would turn green once again, and the shrubbery leaves would glisten, dark and fresh, in the morning.

'The rains,' she whispered softly to herself, half in returning sleep. 'Here come the rains.'

Straight after breakfast Ned came round for Ione. They were going out to collect jumble together.

He stood in the steadily pouring rain, in a large puddle, looking quite extraordinary even for him, and he wasn't known in the village as a natty dresser. He had on a huge flapping bicycle cape made from shiny black rubber, so loose and long on him that it looked rather as if he had chosen to deck himself out for the day in a smallish tent. Its capacious hood covered his head and most of his face, making him appear strangely sinister, like a lanky grave-digger, or one of Dracula's more secretive henchmen. In one hand he carried a cracked and rusting old hand-bell, and in the other a length of frayed rope which trailed round the corner, and at which he tugged fruitlessly from time to time.

'What have you got at the end of that rope?' Ione asked him, staying safe under the porch while she buttoned her school raincoat right up to her chin, and pulled her rainhat on tightly.

'My hand-cart,' said Ned. 'We need a cart. We can't be forever trudging to and from the church hall with small armfuls. We are going to be efficient about this jumble collecting.' He hitched his hood up even further over his face till only his mouth and chin could be seen. 'We are going to boil down what has been treated hithertofore as an inept art into one of the more exact sciences.' He opened the gate for her courteously, and then nearly ran her down with his little wooden wagon. 'I intend to write a short paper on my findings, to be published in *Science Quarterly*. I think I may break new ground.'

'I think you have already,' said Ione, looking behind her. 'Your cart's wheels have shredded our lawn.'

'Sorry,' said Ned.

They began at the east end of the village street, according to a plan that Ned had conceived whilst shaving.

Ned took the lead. He hauled along the cart, by the rope that went over his shoulder, stooping more than usual, and limping and hobbling horribly, ending each stride with a shudder, frightful to look at.

'What on earth are you doing?' asked Ione.

'Trust me,' said Ned, over his shoulder. 'Just trust me. We've only got till Saturday. If we do it your way, the normal way – "Please can we have something for our jumble sale, Ma'am?" – all we'll end up with is two broken fish-slices and a lot of promises. So just keep quiet and trust me.'

He staggered along the dripping, glistening street,

splashing through the puddles, and as he went, he tolled his bell slowly and sonorously.

'Bring out your dead!' he shouted through the steady rain, in a forced cracked voice, with an odd rustic accent. 'Bring 'em out, ladies. Bring out your dead!'

He kept it up all the way along the street – the cart rumbling along loudly in his wake – and half of the way back.

After a while, Ione noticed that several of the lace curtains in the cottage windows had begun to twitch. Curious faces appeared at the upstairs windows of the larger houses, and aproned mothers, dusters in hand or babies on hips, sidled noiselessly into half-opened doorways.

'Bring out your dead!' bellowed Ned, even more loudly. 'Come on. Can't leave 'em rotting. Bring 'em all out!'

Suddenly a bedroom window just above him opened up with a piercing creak.

'Is that you, Ned Hump?' shouted Nurse Hicks, leaning out dangerously far.

'Bain't be no Ned 'Ump around 'ere what I know of,' Ned bellowed back up at her. 'There were one Lord Edward 'Ump, and a fine, strapping, handsome, charming, intelligent lad he were, to be sure. A joy to 'is family and a credit to the county. But 'e's been dead and gone a week or more. Why, I took 'is fair young body away to the pits myself, on this very cart. 'Ee was one of the first to go.' He shook his

89

head sadly from side to side, and waggled a finger at Nurse Hicks. 'It's always the cream as gets skimmed off first, so they do say.'

Nurse Hicks stared down at him, speechless.

More doors opened. More pairs of eyes stared. Ione was torn between blushing and giggling. In the end, she did both.

'What *is* he doing?' someone shouted from away down the street. 'Is that Ned Hump? What on earth does he *want*?'

'What do you want?' someone closer shouted at Ned.

'Your dead,' said Ned, as he limped and hobbled back down the street. 'Bring out your dead!'

'You'll get no sense out of *him*,' said Nurse Hicks. 'He's a right loon. Ask Ione. Ione, whatever is he up to? What does he want?'

'Jumble,' said Ione, pulling herself together fast, and speaking as clearly as she could through tears of laughter. 'He's collecting jumble. He wants jumble for Saturday's jumble sale.'

'Oh, for heaven's *sake*!' said Nurse Hicks, totally exasperated, and she slammed the bedroom window shut.

Ned parked the cart in the middle of the street, half-way from each end, and waited, tolling his bell.

Sure enough, his scheme had worked. He had caught the whole street's attention within minutes. One by one, the doors opened wider, and the jumble began to pour out.

Ned and Ione ran here and there, up and down the street, from one side of the road to the other, from door to door, taking the proffered goods in armfuls, bringing them back to the cart and slipping them under the tarpaulin Ned had left on the top, to keep everything dry.

They were given egg-cups in sets of three, old seventy-eight r.p.m. records sung by Caruso, a hand-loom in several heavy pieces which Ned, after his promise of a few days before, felt obliged to carry to the cart for Ione. They staggered under the weight of armfuls of magazines, children's outgrown clothes, discarded bedspreads and a set of matching bird-cages. Ned was given eighteen pounds of chutney in large jars. 'Too hot for us, love,' said the lady who pressed the carton on him. 'Sell it as curry paste I should, if I were you.'

Ione trapped her finger in a large toy garage, and stained the front of her raincoat with some uncapped yellow ochre from a box of ancient oil colours. She counted four sieves, nearly a dozen broken fish-slices, and scores of paperbacks.

'All this stuff,' she breathed, marvelling at the amount and the variety. 'All this *stuff*.'

And on the door of every house from which they had been handed jumble, Ned chalked a large cross.

'I suppose you think that's very funny indeed,' said the choirmaster's wife, who used to teach history at the primary school until she quarrelled badly with Miss Casterpool.

Within ten minutes, every door on the street except one bore the tell-tale mark of generosity. And while everybody in the street watched from their doorsteps or windowsills or from behind their curtains, Ned bore down on one door with his noisy cart and his noisy bell.

He planted himself just before the doorstep, and rapped the knocker, long and loud.

'Come on out, you old bat,' he shouted. 'Show your face and hand over your jumble.'

The door opened a crack.

'You go away, Ned Hump,' came a high, spirited voice. 'You go away and boil your head.'

Ned clanged his bell furiously.

'If you don't hand over some jumble before I count to twenty,' he yelled, 'I'm going to write a *very rude word* on your nice door in my fluorescent, indelible chalk. And you'd better start jumble-hunting right now, you mean-spirited old bat, because I'm starting to count.'

He began counting aloud, slowly and menacingly.

The whole street waited, breathless with excitement.

He had reached seventeen before the door opened again, just half-way, and Ermyntrude Curmudgeon hobbled out on to her doorstep, wagging her head wildly from side to side, and waving a coal shovel threateningly in Ned's direction.

'Lovely,' said Ned, reaching out for it. 'Very nice. Most acceptable. Hand it over.'

'You keep off, Ned Hump,' croaked Ermyntrude Curmudgeon, livid with rage. 'This is to hit you with, not to give you.'

'Come on, you old troll,' Ned wheedled. 'What's a bit of old jumble going to set you back? One cluttered cupboard, that's all. Come on. Listen, I'll be reasonable. I'm not after anything fancy. I'll settle for two torn antimacassars and a plastic doily.'

'I haven't got any jumble,' the old lady insisted in her cracked, penetrating voice. 'And even if I did have, I'd die rather than give any of it to the likes of you.'

'You'll have to make biscuits, then,' said Ned, 'for the food stall.'

She stared at him, horrified, completely taken aback. Her mouth dropped open.

'Biscuits?' she whispered. '*Me?*'

'Yes,' said Ned firmly. 'It's up to you. There are going to be no free-loaders at Saturday's sale. It's either jumble or home-made biscuits or you can't come.'

A tremor of horror ran down the street. Ione could hear it, like a chill, fast breath.

'Can't come? *Can't come?*'

'That's right,' Ned repeated. 'We won't let you come. We'll throw you out. You won't be allowed to so much as finger the cracked plates. If you won't contribute then you can't come round on Saturday, scavenging off the rest of us busy citizenry. Being eighty-eight is no excuse at all. None. The same rules go for you as for the rest of us. No jumble, no sale, and that's that.'

There was dead silence for several moments.

It was so quiet, each raindrop seemed to make an audible splash. The people watched and waited, waited and watched, spellbound.

Ned shrank inside his cloak, as he, too, waited. Ermyntrude Curmudgeon stood perfectly still.

Then, without warning, she turned on her heel and disappeared back into her house, leaving the door ajar.

Not a soul spoke. Even the babies were quiet.

Within a minute, she was back. She appeared on her doorstep like a witch in a fury. She flung a complete set of plastic measuring spoons at Ned's head, catching him on the ear, and then tossed a large darned tablecloth and several stained napkins on to the cart. Then she went back inside, slamming the door viciously behind her.

Ned turned and picked up the plastic measuring spoons. He wiped the mud off them with his fingers and handed them to Ione, who put them neatly in a teapot on the top of the cart. Then, as loud, ringing applause broke out from every doorway in the street, Ned bowed low, two or three times.

'Come along, Ione,' he said. 'We are falling rather badly behind our schedule.'

94

She followed him, as he limped and stooped down the wet street, tolling his bell, and shouting, 'Bring out your dead!'

The applause lasted until they had turned the corner.

Here, Ned turned to her, and pushed the hood back off his face for a moment.

'See?' he said to her proudly. '*See?*'

9

They worked all morning without a break, collecting jumble. Each time the cart filled to overflowing with toasters, gardening tools, plant pots, kettles and mousetraps, Ned would haul it off to the church hall and tip it in unruly piles on the cloakroom floor.

They would lean against the wall for a while, admiringly, and then trundle the cart back for more. By mid-afternoon they had gathered together an astonishing amount of jumble, and both of them were exhausted.

'It would have been far easier with three,' Ned said at one point, as they staggered to the cart under the weight of a large wooden dog-kennel that Mrs Asprey had kindly donated. 'Caroline should have come with us. She promised yesterday that she would. But when I reminded her this morning, she said she had something else more important to do.'

He shook his head forlornly. Sometimes it seemed

to him that Caroline always wriggled out of any job, however important it might be, that would make her get cold and wet or scruffy. That was one quality in Ione that he had really come to admire, he reflected. She didn't mind getting cold and wet and scruffy. He peered at her more closely through the rain. She looked far too cold, he thought. Frightfully wet and downright filthy.

'That's it,' he said decisively. 'That's the lot. I'm not doing any more. We'll just take this lot back and then we'll go home.'

Ione pushed her rainhat back a little. Her face was very pale and strained.

'There's only two more streets to do,' she said wistfully.

All through the day, whenever what she was carrying had been heavy and awkward, or had trapped her fingers, whenever she stepped into a puddle that was deeper than she expected, and the water had run over into her shoes, making her socks squelch miserably, whenever the rain forced itself down her neck, or her hands had stiffened from cold, or she had felt the tears of exhaustion and exasperation rise in her eyes, she had brought back in her mind the picture of the other, darker Ned standing on the edge of his wide, hot, barren, lifeless plain, waiting and wondering what on earth he was going to do.

The picture came to mind now, and she stood still, drenched by the rain, absorbed.

'Enough is enough,' said Ned firmly.

He took her hand and led her back towards the church, and the little wooden wagon rumbled and splashed along behind them, as it had all day.

Stuck up in the oak tree that overlooked the school playground, unable to get down again, Caroline heard, above the shouts and yells and screams of the home-going children, the noisy rumble of the cart.

She shifted the gobstopper she was sucking – neither as large, nor as colourful as the old variety, she noticed – from one bulging cheek to the other.

Rescue, she thought. At last, I shall be rescued.

She had been stuck up the tree well over an hour and a half, since the children's mid-afternoon break. She was damp, chilled and cramped.

She looked down through the thick, leafy mass of branches from which she could not descend without help, and saw her husband and Ione approaching, slowly, hand in hand.

'Ned,' she called out. '*Ned!*'

The gobstopper made her voice thick and un-recognisable.

'Ned!'

Ned Hump stopped dead in his tracks on the pavement. He dropped Ione's hand. He stared up.

He had heard his name, but he could see no one. He looked up beyond the oak tree into the sky, baffled.

'Ned,' he heard the strange voice again. 'Ned!'

'Yes, God?' said Ned.

Caroline, from her perch in the tree, saw his blank, staring face.

'I need help, Ned,' she called down to him.

'Anything you say, God,' said Ned, dropping to his knees in the gutter.

Ione gazed up, too, dazed with tiredness and surprise.

Caroline, exasperated, spat out her gobstopper. It landed just beside the kneeling Ned, shattering into a hundred brightly coloured fragments.

'Look, Ione,' Ned said. 'A thunderbolt.'

Ione burst out laughing.

The voice that now came from above was quite recognisable. Irritable, edgy and unmistakably Caroline's.

'Get off your knees this minute, Ned Hump and stop your fooling. Help me down out of this stupid tree.'

Ned rose to his feet.

'The lady moves in mysterious ways, her wonders to perform,' he observed softly to Ione. Then he stepped beneath the branches that were shaking and rustling just above his head.

From out of the tree, a pair of large red wellington boots descended, slowly, a few inches.

Ned reached up and seized them. He directed one on to each shoulder.

'Steady,' he warned her. 'Don't let go yet, love. Steady.'

'Ned,' hissed Caroline from between clenched

teeth. 'I am in no position up here to be choosy.'

Ione watched, fascinated, as Ned began to sway one way, and Caroline's legs, above him, began to sway another.

'Easy,' Ned shouted. 'If you could just slide down *slowly*.'

'*Help!*' shrieked Caroline, panicking. 'Don't drop me, Ned. Hold *on*.'

Ned held on. It was the worst thing he could have done. Caroline wriggled and flailed and thrashed and fought, and as the branches she was depending upon cracked and gave, she fell down on top of him and they ended up on the street in a chaotic, muddy heap.

In his right hand, Ned still clutched one of Caroline's red wellington boots tightly. He was winded and grazed.

'Oaf!' said Caroline. 'Clumsy oaf.'

'Idiot,' Ned returned fondly. 'What on earth were you *doing* up there?'

Without getting up, for she was far too wet and grubby now for it to make any difference, Caroline dug in her pocket and handed him a paper dart.

Raising his eyebrows, he unfolded it.

It was, in fact, a printed notice, printed as Ione, who was looking over his shoulder, immediately recognised, on one of the copy machines Caroline often used for her father's work. It had the large fuzzy blank patch in the top left-hand corner that people so often complained about. It said, printed in large, round, easy small letters:

Come and get a big red helium balloon. Come to the church hall on Saturday at half-past two. Tell your friends. Lots of toys and games. Bring all your pocket money. Don't forget.

Underneath, there was a copy of Ione's drawing of Miss Casterpool being swept up and away by a crowd of helium balloons.

'I sent dozens of them over,' said Caroline proudly. 'I became really rather skilled at it. I could even hit people who hadn't got one yet. I think all of the little brats got one in the end. They had a great time. They chased about after them, getting all over-excited and making a dreadful din. The biggies read them out to the babies, and explained what helium balloons were. None of them would go in at the end of break, they were so over-excited. They kept running out of line to pick up the spares. Miss Casterpool had to come out and shriek at them.' Caroline smiled warmly at the memory. 'She went wild. She was frantic. She kept trying to work out where they were all coming from, but I was much too clever for her.'

She explored a sore place on her cheek gently with her fingers.

'Not clever enough to get down again, though,' she ended, forlornly. 'I'm going to get a terrible bruise. I shall be quite disfigured.'

She stood up.

'Can we go home now, Ned?' she asked him plaintively. 'Have you two finished, too?' She shivered. 'I've been up there ever since lunchtime and I'm so very cold and wet.'

Ned gazed at her, full of love and admiration. Then he kissed her. She was cold; she was wet; and she was gloriously, gloriously scruffy.

10

Saturday morning dawned bright and beautiful. Ione lay in her bed, watching the sunlight sweep across her bedroom wall; and stretching out her toes between the tangled sheets, she let herself bathe in visions of prancing, dancing coins, fluttering pound notes and the occasional nice green cheque.

She purred softly. It was going to be a splendid, wonderful day.

Ned got up early and walked over the lawn to the vicarage, interrupting the vicar at his breakfast. The vicar was spooning lemon curd on to his toast and listening to the news on the radio.

'We need the church hall keys,' Ned told him. 'All our jumble is still outside in the cloakroom. We have to get it in and set it all out on the trestle tables by two o'clock.'

The vicar lifted his head. He hated being bothered

at breakfast. And Ned had talked right through the price index figures he had wanted to catch.

'Keys?' he said irritably. 'I haven't got the keys. And the church hall is all locked up this weekend. Midway & Sons painted the walls yesterday, and they're coming back on Monday to varnish all the woodwork.' He took a large bite of toast and talked through it. 'They always take the keys away with them when they paint the church hall. They have done ever since the Brownies got in too early one time to rehearse *Night of the Living Dead*, and covered the walls with grubby little fingerprints before the paint dried.'

Ned sat down heavily at the breakfast table.

'Oh,' he said. 'Oh, dear.'

He reached out, unthinking, for the lemon curd pot and dipped his finger in. 'Nice,' he said, licking appreciatively. 'Not too sweet.'

The vicar prised the pot from between Ned's fingers and placed it safely out of reach behind the salt cellar.

'You'll have to postpone it,' he said. 'You should never have chosen today in the first place. It's most irregular. You should always ask first. It's *my* job to arrange all these things, after all,' he added petulantly, wiping his mouth with his napkin. 'That's exactly what I'm here for.'

'Is it?' asked Ned, with quickening interest. 'Is it really? I had no idea. I thought you were here for baptisms and weddings and funerals and visiting the sick and suchlike. I thought jumble sale arrangements and church hall redecorating was just a sideline of yours. I had no idea that was exactly what you were here for.'

The vicar, irritated, rose and pushed his chair in neatly under the table. There was a strong anticlerical streak in Ned Hump, he reflected, that he had never much cared for.

'You'll have to sort it out yourself,' he said. 'I'm off to a Conference. We all are. All the clergy, including the Bishop himself, are meeting at Rutherstrop today to discuss the changes in the tax laws.'

'Heavens above,' said Ned respectfully.

The vicar picked up his car keys and left in a small huff.

Ned pushed the salt aside, retrieved the lemon curd pot, and sat there quietly for a while, spooning curd into his mouth with his finger, thinking.

Caroline was overtaken by the vicar on the wicked left-hand bend that led into the narrow bridge over Rutherstrop river, where the accident black spot warning sign used to be before the juggernaut ripped it out, jack-knifing into the weir. She wondered why he was in such a hurry. She herself was driving Nurse Hicks' old Anglia, which hadn't been able to go very fast ever since it completely overheated on the way to Eveling General, the night young Geoffrey Heath was born. So Caroline had plenty of time to gaze out at the passing countryside – considerably fresher looking since the heavy rain she thought – and at the steadily rising white mists that presaged a glorious day.

She was driving to *Novelties Incorporated & Fairground Supplies*. It was hidden away behind the bone factory and took quite some time to find.

'I want a helium balloon gas thing,' she told the man in the warehouse. 'And hundreds of balloons. And thirty novelties, for prizes.'

The man yawned and scratched at his ear. A pencil that had been wedged behind it fell off, on to the floor. He picked it up and began writing yesterday's date on a bright yellow invoice slip. 'Sweet little bath ducks that float or nasty little skeleton key rings that squirt water in your face?' he asked her, yawning again.

Caroline thought about it.

On the one hand, none of the little children she had seen the day before in the playground had looked old enough to have things that locked. On the other hand, none of them looked that partial to baths, either. There again, a lot of the Brownies might come.

'Nasty little skeleton key rings that squirt water in your face,' she said.

The man showed her how to fill the balloons from the gas cylinder, and instructed her in a faster and better way to knot them.

'You're going to break every single one of your

pretty nails today,' he warned her, with gloomy satisfaction.

Caroline looked down at her purple, glistening fingertips.

'Oh, well,' she sighed. 'It's a very worthy cause.'

He helped her load all her stuff into the back of the car. 'I'll give you a tip,' he said kindly, just before she drove off. 'A rule of thumb, as it were. If they pop or lose them the minute they get them, give them another free. If they come back later with a sob-story, however convincing, make them pay again. It's the only way.'

'Wise,' said Caroline. 'Very wise. Thank you.'

She drove back to the village, humming.

Ione pushed open the door of the toolshed. The wood felt soft and damp and half-rotten against her fingertips, and she wrinkled her nose against the thick, musty smell inside.

She was looking for her doll's house. She wanted to give something to the jumble sale, something from her. She had already put a few books and some old toys into a cardboard box; but none of that was worth more than a few pennies. She wanted to give something that would make up a sizeable bit of the bullock when it was sold, and she knew that her doll's house was the only thing she had.

It was still there, where she had thought it would be, beside the unicycle in the dark, back corner, which the light from the grimy window entirely failed to reach. It was painted white, with a peaked high red roof, and a hinged front. There were roses, little fat globules of hard scarlet paint, over the door, on finely drawn creepers. There were tiny black metal shutters. The windows opened and the door latched. The rooms were small, delicate and beautifully painted. Each of the bedrooms even had a fireplace with a mantelpiece, and the staircase had banisters as delicate as matchsticks.

It was empty of furniture now. Ione had no idea where all the furniture had gone. It was a long time since she had played with it.

Kneeling, she ran her fingertips over the dust that lay in a thin film over the roof, and she fiddled with the upstairs windows. She did not open it. She wasn't sure that she could give it away if she looked at it too closely. It had been very dear to her once.

As she lifted it off the floor, she heard a clatter from behind, and a tiny red tin trowel fell out from the shelf of a broken bookcase against which the doll's house had been carelessly jammed. It fell at her feet.

Ione put the doll's house down on the hood of the lawn mower and stooped to pick up the little red trowel. She thought back to what Mr Hooper had said about her mother. Holding it tightly in her hand, she wondered.

Then, leaving the door ajar for when she returned to fetch the doll's house, she took the trowel away with her, across the lawn to the summer-house.

Her papers still lay scattered on the flagstones. A lot of them were wet. Damp patches still darkened the floor after the rain, and the spider had gone from his web.

Ione stood in the middle of her summer-house, looking around. There was nowhere to put the trowel or the papers. Nowhere. There was nowhere to keep anything. She'd never had anything to keep in there before. She thought she might ask Ned to help her carry in a large box and a table later, when there was more time. She thought they might come in very useful in the future, whenever she was busy with things. But now she just gathered the pamphlets up into a tidy pile and put the little red tin trowel down on the top, to keep them there.

Just as she rose to her feet, a light breeze blew in through the open lattices, rustling the papers under the trowel softly.

Why don't they tell you things? Ione said to herself, as she gently pulled the door closed behind her. Why do you have to hear quite by chance the things you always needed to know?

11

By the time Ione reached the churchyard, carrying her doll's house, Ned had been busy for an hour. He had set up at least a third of the jumble.

Ione stared.

There was jumble all over the graves. Old garden equipment lay neatly against Captain Flook's pillar. Martha Cuddlethwaite's grave was covered in old, battered kitchen equipment. All the foodstuffs were stacked neatly upon Thomas Munch. The war memorial was knee-deep in toys, and baby clothes were draped tastefully from the low hanging branches of the cypresses.

'Come along,' said Ned briskly, hauling a large hairy rug over to the church steps. 'We haven't got all day. I want you to put all the ornaments on Theresa Cunningham while I finish stacking the books on the Hobsons.'

'You *can't*, Ned,' Ione cried out, horrified. 'It's

sacrilege.'

'Nonsense,' said Ned.

'Heresy, then,' Ione insisted. 'It's something dreadful, anyhow.'

'Rubbish,' said Ned. 'Don't be mediaeval.' He waved an arm airily around. 'They might as well make themselves useful, for once,' he told her. 'They just lie around all day, after all. It'll bring a bit of purpose into their lives. I mean deaths.'

'You're so *bad*,' said Ione. 'I never met anyone who could be as *bad* as you can be when you try.'

But she set to work obediently all the same.

By noon, they had everything almost straight. Caroline had taken over the pricing, sticking neat little white labels on everything in sight. Ione took over the job of guessing what things were, and where they should go, and Ned found a large red tin box to keep all the money in.

He strode around the graves looking for somewhere to set up the cash desk.

'Here's a good one,' he called out at last. Ione came over to look. Hidden in the weeds was a low, flat grave, about the height of a coffee table. Little creepers had almost covered one end, and there was a faint stain of moss over the surface. But the inscription could still be read, quite clearly, on its face:

> *Death is a debt to nature due,*
> *Which I have paid, and so must you.*

'Fine,' she told him, pleased. 'Perfect.'

She was getting altogether taken with the idea now, Ned saw.

It came as a surprise to them when Officer Munch interrupted them, shortly after lunchtime. He leaned over the wall, looking hot and cross in his dark blue uniform.

'What's all this?' he said to them. 'What's going on here? You can't do this. You can't hold a jumble sale in a graveyard. The very *idea!*'

They looked at one another silently, each hoping that one of the others would explain.

Officer Munch strode in through the wicket gate past the notice-board, and began to walk around the churchyard in a frenzy, staring at everything and outraged at everything he stared at.

He drew up short at the foodstuffs, and pointed.

'You can't *do* this!' he shouted at them. 'You just can't *do* this. That's my grandfather, that is. What's he doing with all that jam and cake all over him? Clear him up at once!'

'He won't mind,' Ned explained patiently. 'He won't even know. He's dead.'

'I know he's dead,' said Officer Munch quite furious. 'That's why he's buried here. He's buried here to Rest In Peace, that's what he's buried here for. Not to be bargained over and shopped off, by the likes of you.'

'Now, now,' said Caroline. 'There's no need to take on like this.'

Officer Munch glared fiercely at Caroline, whom

he had until then ignored. Things were clearly going from bad to worse. Ione took a deep breath. She was thinking fast.

This had been a very important two weeks for Ione, in more ways than she had at first realised. She had put a great deal of thought and a great deal of effort into this jumble sale, and it was the first big thing that she had ever really done. She was not going to give it up now. She couldn't. Everything would turn into a waste if she didn't save it at once. All her work and caring would go straight down the drain. The other, darker Ned might lose his bullock; but Ione would lose something too, she now saw. A gift quite as important and valuable to her as the bullock was going to be to him. She would lose all the confidence that had been quietly, steadily, secretly growing inside her that she, Ione Muffet, was capable of real achievements too: that there was always, from now on, going to be more to living for her than just sitting around letting life slide past her.

She could see she had a lot of serious thinking to do – about eavesdropping, which was a part of what had got her started on all this, and about lying, which she was sure could carry it through even now. Ione promised herself that she would think about those things, quietly, for herself, just as soon as she had the time. But right now she was going to take responsibility for rescuing her plans. If trouble followed, then let it. It was worth it to her. And she would try her hardest never to get in this sort of mess again.

Stepping forward, she turned up her clear, innocent face to Officer Munch.

'It's perfectly all right,' she told him calmly. 'There's no problem at all. We can hold the jumble sale in the graveyard. We have special permission from the Bishop.'

Ned's mouth dropped open.

Caroline said, 'Ooooh,' softly, under her breath.

Officer Munch looked down at her, astonished and partly disbelieving.

'You can phone him if you like,' Ione continued coolly. 'To check.'

'Phone the Bishop?'

Officer Munch was appalled by the sheer cheek of the suggestion.

'Certainly,' said Ned, catching on fast. 'I'll dial for you.'

And he led them all, in a little procession, between the graves, over the vicarage lawn, and into the vicar's kitchen.

He took the phone off the hook and dialled a number.

Ione stood by, watching. It was her idea, but she was very glad indeed that Ned had taken over.

When the ringing at the other end of the line was interrupted by the lifting of the receiver, Ned spoke at once.

'Sorry to disturb you, Your Worship,' said Ned,

'but we have a bit of a problem here.'

'Is that you, Ned?' said Professor Muffet, at the other end of the line. He wished he hadn't answered the phone. He was busy threading a new punch tape into his braille typewriter. It had already become tangled, and he was getting irritable. He was in no mood for one of Ned's jokes.

'Yes, Your Worship,' said Ned. 'Yes, it is. And we have a problem. Officer Munch would like to be assured that Ione Muffet, a young lady of this parish, does, indeed, have Your Worship's most gracious permission to hold her Grand Jumble Sale in St Edmund's churchyard. On the graves,' he added as an afterthought, in case there should be any confusion. 'Shall I put Officer Munch on the line, Your Worship?'

'No,' said Professor Muffet, fast.

'Here he is, then,' said Ned sweetly, and he handed the receiver to Officer Munch, who wiped his palms on the seat of his trousers before taking it gingerly. He held it a safe and respectful couple of inches away from his ear. He could hear strange noises issuing from the other end of the line. The connections do get worse and worse, he thought to himself.

In his study, Professor Muffet was having a wordless, furious tantrum. The things he *gets* me into, he said to himself, wild with anger, sweeping a pile of papers on to the floor. The *trouble* he can be, he added, stamping viciously on the rug. I shall *never*

forgive him, he promised himself, tugging freneti-
cally at his thinning hair. I'll *kill* him, he finished
up, clenching his fists.

'Your Worship . . . ?' began Officer Munch tentatively.

Professor Muffet consoled himself with the thought
that it was a very worthy cause. He calmed himself
down at once, just enough to cope.

'Ah, Munch,' Professor Muffet boomed in his most
bishoply tones, down the phone. 'So good of you to
ring. Most responsible of you to think of checking.
I'm extremely pleased with you.'

In the vicar's kitchen, Officer Munch stood a little
straighter, and began to feel better.

'Everything is perfectly in order,' Professor Muffet
went on. 'Everyone may carry on. The whole enter-
prise will bring great credit on the parish of St
Edmund's. And it will be appreciated in Higher
Quarters, you may be sure of that.' His voice trailed
to a halt. Since he had no very clear idea of what
was going on down there in the church grounds, he
didn't want to get in too deep, in case he set a foot
wrong.

Officer Munch remained silent at his end of the
phone.

Oh, well, thought Professor Muffet, in for a
penny, in for a pound.

'There may even be a photograph,' he ended up
blandly. 'I hope to see you in it. You are a credit to
the Force.'

Officer Munch swallowed. His heart was very full.

'Thank you, Your Worship,' he said, and put the phone down, gently and respectfully.

In his study, Professor Muffet cradled the receiver with a bang and went back to his tantrum. But it was no longer a wordless one, and Mandy, overcome with surprise, crept out of the French windows and off into the shrubbery, out of the way.

'That's that, then,' said Ned Hump. 'Back to work, men. It's almost time for the hordes to arrive.'

And they all trooped out of the vicarage. Caroline, Ned and Ione went back to the graveyard, and Officer Munch slipped back home to polish his shoes and his buttons.

There hadn't been a really *nice* photo of him since V.E. Day, he recalled.

12

The jumble sale was a huge success. Everybody said so. There had never been one to match it in the whole of the village's history. It went on for hours and hours and hours.

Almost everything was sold. What could not be sold was given away. 'It's an ecologically sound principle, recycling is,' said Ned, as he handed Ermyntrude Curmudgeon a broken-off spoon and a pot of ancient jam that nobody else had fancied. The jam bore a faint greenish tinge. 'If that doesn't kill you off, you old bat,' he said to her pleasantly, 'then you're immortal.'

'I'll be around to see you hanged, Ned Hump,' she snarled back, and staggered off home, laden with a complete set of new fire irons. 'If I don't do you in myself with these, first.'

Miss Casterpool arrived promptly, and went straight over to the books, stacked neatly upon the

Hobsons. She rooted through each pile briskly, pulling out one book after another, and handing them disdainfully to Ned, who stood attentively behind the grave.

Ned put the books neatly in a cardboard box for her to carry. He thought it was nice of her to have come, after all, and he wanted to be friendly.

'There are thirty-one,' he said, when at last she had checked through every single book pile. 'And that comes to one pound fifty-five pence, but I'm going to let you have them for one pound fifty.'

'I'm certainly not paying you a single penny,' she crowed at him. 'However worthy the cause. These books are all lost, mislaid or stolen school textbooks. Every single one of them bears the county stamp.' She narrowed her cold grey eyes at him suspiciously. 'And I would give a lot to know where they came from.'

'You needn't look at me,' said Ned. '*I* never took them. I never even went to your primary school. I wish I had. But I was educated at home by an extraordinarily beautiful and gifted governess, the natural daughter of an earl. She had golden tresses that fell over my work books in long, soft ringlets, brushing my cheek, and eyes as blue as heaven.' His face took on an expression of rapt remembrance. 'But on my twelfth birthday, she ravished me in the greenhouse and then cut her throat before my very eyes with a pair of gardening shears. So my parents put me in Rutherstrop Technical College.'

Miss Casterpool trembled with shock and rage.

'You're a *monster*,' she whispered at him fiercely. 'An absolute *monster*.'

'Can I carry these to the gate for you?' asked Ned pleasantly. 'Whoops, sorry pardon. *May* I?'

A shiver of scarcely controllable fury passed through Miss Casterpool's body. Several moments passed before she could collect herself sufficiently to turn on her heel and walk away.

The Heaths came, Ione was pleased and relieved to see. They bought the dog-kennel. Mr Heath held it out proudly for his son to peep into.

'There you are, Geoffrey,' he said happily. 'Now you're over your mouth ulcers, we'll get you a puppy and you can catch worms instead.'

Ione giggled, and he turned to look at her. 'I've had your poster up,' he told her. 'And everyone re-marked on how special it was. Buried the hatchet nicely, didn't we?'

'You'll need another one, then,' said Caroline, passing him one around Captain Flook's pillar. 'It's only eighteen pence, because the handle's split.'

'No, thank you,' said Mrs Heath. 'You'd better save it to defend yourself against the vicar when he gets home from his conference and sees all this mess.'

Ione looked around. There was, indeed, a huge amount of mess. There was a huge amount of money, and a huge amount of mess.

'Lovely,' she said to herself, and sighed happily.

'Lovely.'

The graveyard was covered with price tags. They lay over everything, like confetti. A few tattered and soiled napkins still hung from the yew trees, and the ground was spattered with popped red and yellow and blue and green balloon skins.

'How *noisy* it was,' she breathed, thrilled.

It had, indeed, been noisy. One explosion had followed another, like gunfire. The mothers had remonstrated loudly. The children had howled bitterly.

'Just like V.E. Day,' Officer Munch had said to everyone, admiringly, resplendent in his brushed uniform, gleaming buttons and shiny shoes. He had bought a lovely old doll's house, with roses around the door and a peaked red roof, for his four-year-old grand-daughter's birthday, and Nurse Hicks had taken his photo with the camera she had just bought for seventy-five pence. He was happy. He could hardly wait to see the prints.

In a lull at the book grave towards the end of the afternoon, Ned wandered over to his vegetable garden.

'Look,' he called to everyone proudly. 'That rain has done it the world of good. The ground's gone all soggy. I think my turnips may shoot up if it's not too late.'

'Turnips stay down,' said Ione. She was sure someone had told him that before. But he wasn't listening. He had shot off to buy one of the last garden rakes for thirty-five pence.

Towards the very end, Professor Muffet had appeared. Mandy picked a way for him, delicately, through the rising debris. With the help of the choirmaster's wife, Professor Muffet bought a bottle of Worcestershire sauce off Officer Munch's grandfather, an oven glove off Martha Cuddlethwaite, and a bright blue ball for Mandy from the war memorial. Then he settled down against a headstone, to wait for the sale to finish.

Ione sat in the grass, counting the money. Caroline and Ned leaned back together against the trunk of a cypress and watched the let-go balloons career around the sky in the freshening breeze, like faraway coloured dandelion fluff.

'How wonderful it all was,' said Caroline happily. 'It's going to take us *hours* to clean it all up.'

Ned gave Caroline a hard squeeze. There was dirt all over her hands, stickers all over her hair, and the heavy bruise from yesterday on her cheek. Her nails were all broken, from knotting the balloons. She looked positively scruffy again.

'Oh, well,' she whispered to him, seeing his look, and he kissed her.

Two small children rooted through the undergrowth, looking for dropped pennies. Their mothers, tired, laden but contented, called to them from the gate. It had been a grand jumble sale. The best ever.

Ione counted out the piles of money one last time,

and tipped them, one by one, into the red cash box.

'One hundred and two pounds, sixty pence,' she said triumphantly. 'Why, that's very nearly *two* bullocks.'

She looked around at them all hopefully.

'It is only seven pounds short,' agreed Caroline.

A silence fell.

Everyone stared at Professor Muffet, as if by sheer chance. Even Mandy grew uncomfortable, and shuffled around on her haunches against the headstone.

'Don't,' said Professor Muffet, pushing her down flat. 'Have some sense of where you are.'

Nobody else spoke, and after a few moments, Ned began to whistle softly.

'Are you all looking at me?' Professor Muffet demanded hotly at last. 'Why are you all looking at me? You *are* all looking at me, aren't you? I'm being *looked* at.'

'If the cap fits, wear it,' said Caroline.

'What do you want?' Ione's father insisted. 'What are you waiting for?'

'We're waiting for you to do the decent thing,' said Ned.

'What's that?'

'To cough up.'

'*What?* Seven *pounds?* All by *myself?* Why *should* I?'

'Don't be cheap, please,' said Ned.

They all fell, once again, into another, equally uncomfortable silence.

After a while, Professor Muffet asked:

'Why does it have to be exactly a hundred and nine pounds, sixty? Why can't Ione send in what she's got? They can buy the first bullock, and then they'll have some cash left over to buy it some food.'

'Or a pretty bell to go around its neck,' said Caroline sarcastically.

Professor Muffet shifted uneasily against the cool stone.

'Maybe they could get a baby one with the leftover pounds,' he suggested.

'Or a deformed one,' said Ned. 'I bet a three-legged bullock can be had for peanuts out there in India.'

'Don't be silly,' said Ione. 'It would never stay up.'

Ned stared at her. But since she was staring back at him, equally forcefully, he changed his mind and carried on staring at Professor Muffet instead.

'We're still waiting,' he said sternly.

Professor Muffet thought. Then he went all cunning.

'Couldn't we split it between us?' he wheedled. 'One pound, seventy pence each. That wouldn't be too much of a blow.'

'Look,' said Ned patiently. 'Try thinking of it this way. If you cough up the extra seven, that means the second one is more your bullock than anyone else's. So you can choose which bit you want. Have the head. The head's the best bit. That's the bit that counts.'

'Not with bullocks,' said Ione.

'It's brawn they want the bullock for, not brains,' agreed Caroline.

Ned waved at them to keep quiet.

'If you have the head,' he said to Professor Muffet, who was still patting nervously at the pocket in which he kept his cheque-book, 'then you can choose its name. See?'

'You could give it *your* name,' said Ione.

'Bullock Muffet,' Ned said in a rich and resonant voice. 'Bullock Muffet. Now that's a fine name for an animal.'

'It is, isn't it?' said Professor Muffet, pleased all at once with the idea. 'It does sound grand, doesn't it?'

'It certainly does,' Ned said firmly. 'And that settles it, then. You can pay by cash or cheque, as you prefer.'

Professor Muffet reached resignedly for his cheque-book, and handed it to Ione, who borrowed a pen from Caroline and wrote in everything before passing it back to her father for him to sign.

Professor Muffet signed with slightly more of a flourish than usual. He was very taken indeed with the idea of a bullock, a huge lumbering tough bullock, rambling around some hot plain in India, bearing his name.

He ripped out the cheque, and held it out to

them. Ned took it, and handed it, with a low bow, to Ione.

'There you are, Ione,' he said. 'Congratulations. You did it.'

Ione smiled up at him. He had been such a great help. She turned to smile at Caroline. Towards the end she had been invaluable, too. Then she slipped her hand into her father's, and together they set off down the gravel path towards the church gate.

Every now and again, on the short walk back home, Professor Muffet squeezed his daughter's hand proudly. From time to time he muttered, 'Bullock Muffet,' to himself softly, under his breath.

Ione walked home by his side in a daze of pride and delight, carrying the cash box. The other, darker Ned would not have long to wait now. The rains would fall where he lived, too, in the end, and his land would be tilled and planted. Later, his family would stuff themselves stupid with the long-hoped-for grain.

Ione had plenty of things she should think about. And she would, but not now – not today.

She looked up and around her happily. All along the way, caught and tangled in the horse chestnut trees her mother had planted, the gorgeous fat helium balloons from her jumble sale strained in the wind to escape, and sail gloriously up into the sky.

also available
by Anne Fine

The
Summer-House
Loon

'Ione had swung round, astonished, when she first heard the strange voice. Now she was staring, wide-eyed, at the interloper ...'

Being alone every summer since she can remember, her blind father always locked in his study, Ione is looking for excitement. When she is disturbed in her summer-house by the student Ned Hump, she has no idea what consequences this chance meeting will have ...

The first story about Ione and Ned.

A selected list of titles available from Teens · Mandarin

While every effort is made to keep prices low, it is sometimes necessary to increase prices at short notice. Teens · Mandarin Paperbacks reserve the right to show new retail prices on covers which may differ from those previously advertised in the text or elsewhere.

The prices shown below were correct at the time of going to press.

All these books are available at your bookshop or newsagent, or can be ordered direct from the publisher. Just tick the titles you want and fill in the form below.

Teens · Mandarin Paperbacks, Cash Sales Department PO Box 11, Falmouth, Cornwall TR10 9EN

Please send cheque or postal order, no currency, for purchase price quoted and allow the following for postage and packing:

UK 55p for the first book, 22p for the second book and 14p for each additional book ordered to a maximum charge of £1.75.

BFPO and Eire 55p for the first book, 22p for the second book and 14p for each of the next seven books, thereafter 8p per book.

Overseas Customers £1.00 for the first book, 25p per copy for each additional book.

NAME (Block letters) ....

ADDRESS ....

....